D0677272

# COSMOPOLITANS

## Novels by
# W. SOMERSET MAUGHAM

THE NARROW CORNER
ASHENDEN
THE MOON AND SIXPENCE
MRS CRADDOCK
CAKES AND ALE
THE PAINTED VEIL
OF HUMAN BONDAGE
LIZA OF LAMBETH

## Short Stories

COSMOPOLITANS
FIRST PERSON SINGULAR
THE TREMBLING OF A LEAF
AH KING
THE CASUARINA TREE
EAST AND WEST

## Travel

ON A CHINESE SCREEN
THE GENTLEMAN IN THE PARLOUR
DON FERNANDO
THE LAND OF THE BLESSED VIRGIN

## Plays

FOR SERVICES RENDERED
THE BREADWINNER
THE SACRED FLAME
SHEPPEY
THE CONSTANT WIFE
THE CIRCLE
THE EXPLORER
MRS DOT
OUR BETTERS
A MAN OF HONOUR
PENELOPE
JACK STRAW
LADY FREDERICK
THE TENTH MAN
LANDED GENTRY
THE UNKNOWN
SMITH
THE LAND OF PROMISE

W. Somerset Maugham

# COSMOPOLITANS

DOUBLEDAY, DORAN AND COMPANY, INC.
Garden City, New York
*1937*

PRINTED AT THE *Country Life Press*, GARDEN CITY, N. Y., U. S. A.

# PREFACE

THE LITTLE STORIES in this volume were written on commission. The first was written in 1923; the last, I think, in 1929. When I was in China, meaning to write an account of my journey, I took notes of whatever I saw that excited my interest; but when I came home and read them it seemed to me that they had a vividness that I might easily lose if I tried to elaborate them into a connected narrative. So I changed my mind and decided to publish them as they stood under the title: On a Chinese Screen. Ray Long, who was then editor of the Cosmopolitan Magazine, chanced to read this and it occurred to him that some of my notes might very well be taken for short stories. If you are a story-teller any curious person you meet has a way of suggesting a story, and incidents that to others will seem quite haphazard have a way of presenting themselves to you with the pattern your natural instinct has imposed on them.

Magazine readers do not like starting a story and after reading for a while being told to turn to page a hundred and something. Writers do not like it either, for they think the interruption disturbs the reader and they have an uneasy fear that sometimes he will not take the trouble and so may leave their story unfinished. There is no help for it. Everyone should know that a magazine costs more to produce than it is sold for and could not exist but for the advertisements. The advertisers think that their announcements are more likely to be read if they are on the same page as matter which they modestly, but often mistakenly, think of greater interest. So in the illustrated periodicals it has been found advisable to put the beginning of a story or an article, with the picture that purports to illustrate it, at the beginning and the continuation with the advertisements later on.

Neither readers nor writers should complain. Readers get something for less than cost price, and writers are paid sums for their productions which only the advertisements render possible. They should remember that they are there as baits. Their office is to fill blank spaces and indirectly induce their readers to buy motor accessories, bust bodices and join correspondence courses. Fortunately this need not affect them. The best story from the advertisers' standpoint (and they make their views felt on this question) is the story that gives readers most delight. Ray Long conceived the notion that the readers of the Cosmopolitan would like it if they were given at least one story that they could read without having to hunt for the continuation among the advertisements and he commissioned me to write half a dozen sketches of the same sort as those in On a Chinese Screen. They were to be short enough to print on opposite pages of the magazine and leave plenty of room for illustration.

The sketches I wrote pleased and the commission was renewed. I went on writing them till my natural verbosity got the better of me and I found myself no longer able to keep my stories within the limits imposed upon me. Then I had to stop.

But I think I learned a good deal from the writing of them and I am glad that I wrote them. My difficulty was to compress what I had to tell into a number of words which must not be exceeded and yet leave the reader with the impression that I had told all there was to tell. It was this that made the enterprise amusing. It was also salutary. I could not afford to waste a word. I had to be succinct. I was surprised to find how many adverbs and adjectives I could leave out without any harm to the matter or the manner. One often writes needless words because they give the phrase a better ring. It was very good practice to try to get balance into a sentence without using a word that was not necessary to the sense.

The matter of course had to be chosen with

discretion; it would have been futile to take a theme that demanded elaborate development; and I have a natural predilection for completeness, so that even in the little space at my disposal I wanted my story to have a beginning, a middle and an end. I do not for my own part much care for the shapeless story. To my mind it is not enough when the writer gives you the plain facts seen through his own eye (which means of course that they are not plain facts, but facts distorted by his own idiosyncrasy); I think he should impose upon them a design. Naturally these stories are anecdotes. If stories are interesting and well told they are none the worse for that. The story of the Good Samaritan is an anecdote and a very good one. The anecdote is the basis of fiction. The restlessness of writers forces upon fiction from time to time forms that are foreign to it, but when it has been oppressed for a period by obscurity, propaganda or affectation, it reverts, and returns inevitably to the anecdote.

The University of Columbia a little while ago very kindly sent me a little book entitled Modern Fiction written by two of its professors. I read it with interest and edification. It offers the best guide I have ever met across the fogbound swamps, shining mountains, pleasant oases and dreary deserts of Mr Joyce's Ulysses. It treats of no book that it does not make one wish to read again. It is tolerant, perspicacious and stimulating. But there is one thing about it that very much surprised me. The books of which it treats are discussed in the most improving way. Their technique is acutely analyzed. Their value as psychological, sociological or ethical documents is estimated. But I can find nowhere a reference to their entertainment. So far as I can make out these two professors in all the years during which they have taught the ardent young who attended their lectures never even hinted to them that a novel should be read for fun. The novel may stimulate you to think. It may satisfy your esthetic sense. It may arouse your moral emotions. But if it does not entertain you it is a bad novel. It is merely laziness that induces people to go to novels for instruction on subjects that are the province of experts. There is no short road to knowledge and you will only waste your time if you seek it in a work of fiction. If you are interested in psychology, you had much better read a book on the subject. If you are interested in sociology you had much better go to a sociologist. The technical devices that an author uses to capture your interest are his own affair. Such a one as the "stream of thought" is an amusing trick, but it is of no more real importance than the epistolary style which was in vogue during the eighteenth century. Like that, it is an ingenious expedient to give verisimilitude. To suppose that it can have a scientific value, as some critics have done, is ridiculous. The novelist deals with individual cases which he has chosen to suit his purpose. They may exemplify a rule; they cannot serve to formulate one. The novelist gives you his private view of the universe. He offers you intelligent entertainment; and the first thing you should ask of an entertainment is that it should entertain.

I hope the reader will not think it presumptuous on my part to have touched on these matters of theory in a preface written to introduce a little collection of very short stories. I wish merely to warn him that I ask nothing from him but that he should find them amusing. I think it would be very tiresome to read them at a sitting, but I have a hope that if he reads one or two now and then when he has nothing better to do, he will take the same pleasure in them that was taken by the readers of the Cosmopolitan Magazine when they appeared once every month or so in its pages.

# CONTENTS

Preface *P. v*

Raw Material *P. 1*

Mayhew *P. 7*

German Harry *P. 13*

The Happy Man *P. 19*

The Dream *P. 26*

In a Strange Land *P. 34*

The Luncheon *P. 42*

Salvatore *P. 50*

Home *P. 58*

Mr Know-All *P. 66*

The Escape *P. 77*

A Friend in Need *P. 84*

The Portrait of a Gentleman *P. 92*

The End of the Flight *P. 102*

The Judgement Seat *P. 112*

The Ant and the Grasshopper *P. 120*

French Joe *P. 127*

The Man with the Scar *P. 135*

The Poet *P. 142*

Louise *P. 150*

The Closed Shop *P. 161*

The Promise *P. 176*

A String of Beads *P. 187*

The Bum *P. 198*

Straight Flush *P. 211*

The Verger *P. 221*

The Wash Tub *P. 234*

The Social Sense *P. 248*

The Four Dutchmen *P. 261*

# COSMOPOLITANS

# RAW MATERIAL

I HAVE LONG HAD in mind a novel in which a card-sharper was the principal character; and going up and down the world I have kept my eyes open for members of this profession. Because the notion is prevalent that it is a slightly dishonourable one the persons who follow it do not openly acknowledge the fact. Their reticence is such that it is often not till you have become quite closely acquainted with them, or even have played cards with them two or three times, that you discover in what fashion they earn their living. But even then they have a disinclination to enlarge upon the mysteries of their craft. They have a weakness for passing themselves off for cavalrymen, commercial agents or landed proprietors. This snobbish attitude makes them the most difficult class in the world for the novelist to study. It has been my good fortune to meet a number of these gentlemen and though I have found them affable, obliging and debonair, I have no sooner hinted, however discreetly, at my curiosity (after all purely professional) in the technique of their calling than they have grown shy and uncommunicative. An airy reference on my part to stacking the cards has made them assume immediately the appearance of a clam. I am not easily discouraged, and learning by experience that I could hope for no good results from a direct method, I have adopted the oblique. I have been childlike with them and bland. I have found that they gave me their attention and even their sympathy. Though they confessed honestly that they had never read a word I had written they were interested in the fact that I was a writer. I suppose they felt obscurely that I too followed a calling that the philistine regarded without indulgence. But I have been forced to gather my facts by a bold surmise. It has needed patience and industry.

It may be imagined with what enthusiasm I made the acquaintance a little while ago of two gentlemen who seemed likely to add appreciably to my small store of information. I was travelling from Haiphong on a French liner going East, and they joined the ship at Hong-Kong. They had gone there for the races and were now on their way back to Shanghai. I was going there too and thence to Peking. I soon learned that they had come from New York for a trip, were bound for Peking also, and by a happy coincidence meant to return to America in the ship in which I had myself booked a passage. I was naturally attracted to them, for they were pleasant fellows, but it was not till a fellow-passenger warned me that they were professional gamblers that I settled down to complete enjoyment of their acquaintance. I had no hope that they would ever discuss with frankness their interesting occupation, but I expected from a hint here, from a casual remark there, to learn some very useful things.

One—Campbell was his name—was a man in the late thirties, small but so well built as not to look short, slender, with large, melancholy eyes and beautiful hands. But for a premature baldness he would have been more than commonly good-looking. He was neatly dressed. He spoke slowly, in a low voice, and his movements were deliberate. The other was made on another pattern. He was a big, burly man with a red face and crisp black hair, of powerful appearance, strong in the arm and pugnacious. His name was Peterson.

The merits of the combination were obvious. The elegant, exquisite Campbell had the subtle brain, the knowledge of character, and the deft hands; but the hazards of the card-sharper's life are many, and when it came to a scrap Peterson's ready fist must often have proved invaluable. I do not know how it spread through the ship so quickly that a blow of Peterson's would stretch any man out. But during the short voyage from Hong-Kong to Shanghai they never even suggested a game of cards. Perhaps they had done well during the race week and felt entitled to a holiday. They were certainly enjoying the advantages of not living for the time in a dry country and I do not think I do them an injustice if I say that for the most part they were far from sober. Each one talked little of himself but willingly of the other. Campbell informed me that Peterson was one of the most distinguished mining engineers in New York and Peterson assured me that Campbell was an eminent banker. He said that his wealth was fabulous. And who was I not to accept ingenuously all that was told me? But I thought it negligent of Campbell not to wear jewelry of a more expensive character. It seemed to me that to use a silver cigarette case was rather careless.

I stayed but a day in Shanghai, and though I met the pair again in Peking I was then so much engaged that I saw little of them. I thought it a little odd that Campbell should spend his entire time in the hotel. I do not think he even went to see the Temple of Heaven. But I could quite understand that from his point of view Peking was unsatisfactory and I was not surprised when the pair returned to Shanghai where, I knew, the wealthy merchants played for big money. I met them again in the ship that was to take us across the Pacific and I could not but sympathize with my friends when I saw that the passengers were little inclined to gamble. There were no rich people among them. It was a dull crowd. Campbell indeed suggested a game of poker, but no one would play more than twenty-dollar table stakes, and Peterson, evidently not thinking it worth his while, would not join. Although we played afternoon and evening through the journey he sat down with us only on the last day. I suppose he thought he might just as well make his bar chits, and this he did very satisfactorily in a single sitting. But Campbell evidently loved the game for itself. Of course it is only if you have a passion for the business by which you earn your living that you can make a success of it. The stakes were nothing to him and he played all day and every day. It fascinated me to see the way in which he dealt the cards, very slowly, with his delicate hands. His eyes seemed to bore through the back of each one. He drank heavily, but remained quiet and self-controlled. His face was expressionless. I judged him to be a perfect card player and I wished that I could see him at work. It increased my esteem for him to see that he could take what was only a relaxation so seriously.

I parted with the pair at Victoria and concluded that I should never see them again. I set about sorting my impressions and made notes of the various points that I thought would prove useful.

When I arrived in New York I found an invitation to luncheon at the Ritz with an old friend of mine. When I went she said to me:

"It's quite a small party. A man is coming whom I think you'll like. He's a prominent banker; he's bringing a friend with him."

The words were hardly out of her mouth when I saw coming up to us Campbell and Peterson. The truth flashed across me: Campbell really was an opulent banker; Peterson really was a distinguished engineer; they were not card-sharpers at all. I flatter myself I kept my face, but as I blandly shook hands with them I muttered under my breath furiously:

"Impostors!"

# MAYHEW

THE LIVES OF MOST MEN are determined by their environment. They accept the circumstances amid which fate has thrown them not only with resignation but even with good will. They arc like streetcars running contentedly on their rails and they despise the sprightly flivver that dashes in and out of the traffic and speeds so jauntily across the open country. I respect them; they are good citizens, good husbands, and good fathers, and of course somebody has to pay the taxes; but I do not find them exciting. I am fascinated by the men, few enough in all conscience, who take life in their own hands and seem to mould it to their own liking. It may be that we have no such thing as free will, but at all events we have the illusion of it. At a crossroad it does seem to us that we might go either to the right or to the left, and the choice once made, it is difficult to see that the whole course of the world's history obliged us to take the turning we did.

I never met a more interesting man than Mayhew. He was a lawyer in Detroit. He was an able and a successful one. By the time he was thirty-five he had a large and a lucrative practice, he had amassed a competence, and he stood on the threshold of a distinguished career. He had an acute brain, an attractive personality, and uprightness. There was no reason why he should not become, financially or politically, a power in the land. One evening he was sitting in his club with a group of friends and they were perhaps a little the worse (or the better) for liquor. One of them had recently come from Italy and he told them of a house he had seen at Capri, a house on the hill, overlooking the Bay of Naples, with a large and shady garden. He described to them the beauty of the most beautiful island in the Mediterranean.

"It sounds fine," said Mayhew. "Is that house for sale?"

"Everything is for sale in Italy."

"Let's send 'em a cable and make an offer for it."

"What in heaven's name would you do with a house in Capri?"

"Live in it," said Mayhew.

He sent for a cable form, wrote it out, and dispatched it. In a few hours the reply came back. The offer was accepted.

Mayhew was no hypocrite and he made no secret of the fact that he would never have done so wild a thing if he had been sober, but when he was he did not regret it. He was neither an impulsive nor an emotional man, but a very honest and sincere one. He would never have continued from bravado in a course that he had come to the conclusion was unwise. He made up his mind to do exactly as he had said. He did not care for wealth and he had enough money on which to live in Italy. He thought he could do more with life than spend it on composing the trivial quarrels of unimportant people. He had no definite plan. He merely wanted to get away from a life that had given him all it had to offer. I suppose his friends thought him crazy; some must have done all they could to dissuade him. He arranged his affairs, packed up his furniture and started.

Capri is a gaunt rock of austere outline, bathed in a deep blue sea; but its vineyards, green and smiling, give it a soft and easy grace. It is friendly, remote and debonair. I find it strange that Mayhew should have settled on this lovely island, for I never knew a man more insensible to beauty. I do not know what he sought there: happiness, freedom, or merely leisure; I know what he found. In this place which appeals so extravagantly to the senses he lived a life entirely of the spirit. For the island is rich with historic associations and over it broods always the enigmatic memory of Tiberius the Emperor. From his windows which overlooked the Bay of Naples, with the noble shape of Vesuvius changing in colour with the changing light, Mayhew saw a hundred places that recalled the Romans and the Greeks. The past began to haunt him. All that he saw for the first time, for he had never been abroad before, excited his fancy; and in his soul stirred the creative imagination. He was a man of energy. Presently he made up his mind to write a history. For some time he looked about for a subject, and at last decided on the second century of the Roman Empire. It was little known and it seemed to him to offer problems analogous with those of our own day.

He began to collect books and soon he had an immense library. His legal training had taught him to read quickly. He settled down to work. At first he had been accustomed to foregather in the evening with the painters, writers and such like who met in the little tavern near the piazza, but presently he withdrew himself, for his absorption in his studies became more pressing. He had been accustomed to bathe in that bland sea and to take long walks among the pleasant vineyards, but little by little, grudging the time, he ceased to do so. He worked harder than he had ever worked in Detroit. He would start at noon and work all through the night till the whistle of the steamer that goes every morning from Capri to Naples told him that it was five o'clock and time to go to bed. His subject opened out before him, vaster and more significant, and he imagined a work that would put him for ever beside the great historians of the past. As the years went by he was to be found seldom in the haunts of men. He could be tempted to come out of his house only by a game of chess or the chance of an argument. He loved to set his brain against another's. He was widely read now, not only in history, but in philosophy and science; and he was a skilful controversialist, quick, logical and incisive. But he had good-humour and kindliness; though he took a very human pleasure in victory, he did not exult in it to your mortification.

When first he came to the island he was a big, brawny fellow, with thick black hair and a black beard, of a powerful physique; but gradually his skin became pale and waxy; he grew thin and frail. It was an odd contradiction in the most logical of men that, though a convinced and impetuous materialist, he despised the body; he looked upon it as a vile instrument which he could force to do the spirit's bidding. Neither illness nor lassitude prevented him from going on with his work. For fourteen years he toiled unremittingly. He made thousands and thousands of notes. He sorted and classified them. He had his subject at his finger ends, and at last was ready to begin. He sat down to write. He died.

The body that he, the materialist, had treated so contumeliously took its revenge on him.

That vast accumulation of knowledge is lost for ever. Vain was that ambition, surely not an ignoble one, to set his name beside those of Gibbon and Mommsen. His memory is treasured in the hearts of a few friends, fewer, alas! as the years pass on, and to the world he is unknown in death as he was in life.

And yet to me his life was a success. The pattern is good and complete. He did what he wanted, and he died when his goal was in sight and never knew the bitterness of an end achieved.

# GERMAN HARRY

I WAS IN Thursday Island and I wanted very much to go to New Guinea. Now the only way in which I could do this was by getting a pearling lugger to take me across the Arafura Sea. The pearl fishery at that time was in a bad way and a flock of neat little craft lay anchored in the harbour. I found a skipper with nothing much to do (the journey to Merauke and back could hardly take him less than a month) and with him I made the necessary arrangements. He engaged four Torres Straits islanders as crew (the boat was but nineteen tons) and we ransacked the local store for canned goods. A day or two before I sailed a man who owned a number of pearlers came to me and asked whether on my way I would stop at the island of Trebucket and leave a sack of flour, another of rice, and some magazines for the hermit who lived there.

I pricked up my ears. It appeared that the hermit had lived by himself on this remote and tiny island for thirty years, and when opportunity occurred provisions were sent to him by kindly souls. He said that he was a Dane, but in the Torres Straits he was known as German Harry. His history went back a long way. Thirty years before, he had been an able seaman on a sailing vessel that was wrecked in those treacherous waters. Two boats managed to get away and eventually hit upon the desert island of Trebucket. This is well out of the line of traffic and it was three years before any ship sighted the castaways. Sixteen men had landed on the island, but when at last a schooner, driven from her course by stress of weather, put in for shelter, no more than five were left. When the storm abated the skipper took four of these on board and eventually landed them at Sydney. German Harry refused to go with them. He said that during those three years he had seen such terrible things that he had a horror of his fellow men and wished never to live with them again. He would say no more. He was absolutely fixed in his determination to stay, entirely by himself, in that lonely place. Though now and then opportunity had been given him to leave he had never taken it.

A strange man and a strange story. I learned more about him as we sailed across the desolate sea. The Torres Straits are peppered with islands and at night we anchored on the lea of one or other of them. Of late new pearling grounds have been discovered near Trebucket and in the fall pearlers, visiting it now and then, have given German Harry various necessities so that he has been able to make himself sufficiently comfortable. They bring him papers, bags of flour and rice, and canned meats. He has a whale boat and used to go fishing in it, but now he is no longer strong enough to manage its unwieldy bulk. There is abundant pearl shell on the reef that surrounds his island and this he used to collect and sell to the pearlers for tobacco, and sometimes he found a good pearl for which he got a considerable sum. It is believed that he has, hidden away somewhere, a collection of magnificent pearls. During the war no pearlers came out and for years he never saw a living soul. For all he knew a terrible epidemic had killed off the entire human race and he was the only man alive. He was asked later what he thought.

"I thought something had happened," he said.

He ran out of matches and was afraid that his fire would go out, so he only slept in snatches, putting wood on his fire from time to time all day and all night. He came to the end of his provisions and lived on chickens, fish and coconuts. Sometimes he got a turtle.

During the last four months of the year there may be two or three pearlers about and not infrequently after the day's work they will row in and spend an evening with him. They try to make him drunk and then they ask him what happened during those three years after the two boatloads came to the island. How was it that sixteen landed and at the end of that time only five were left? He never says a word. Drunk or sober he is equally silent on that subject and if they insist grows angry and leaves them.

I forget if it was four or five days before we sighted the hermit's little kingdom. We had been driven by bad weather to take shelter and had spent a couple of days at an island on the way. Trebucket is a low island, perhaps a mile round, covered with coconuts, just raised above the level of the sea and surrounded by a reef so that it can be approached only on one side. There is no opening in the reef and the lugger had to anchor a mile from the shore. We got into a dinghy with the provisions. It was a stiff pull and even within the reef the sea was choppy. I saw the little hut, sheltered by trees, in which German Harry lived, and as we approached he sauntered down slowly to the water's edge. We shouted a greeting, but he did not answer. He was a man of over seventy, very bald, hatchet faced, with a grey beard, and he walked with a roll so that you could never have taken him for anything but a seafaring man. His sunburn made his blue eyes look very pale and they were surrounded by wrinkles as though for long years he had spent interminable hours scanning the vacant sea. He wore dungarees and a singlet, patched, but neat and clean. The house to which he presently led us consisted of a single room with a roof of corrugated iron. There was a bed in it, some rough stools which he himself had made, a table, and his various household utensils. Under a tree in front of it were a table and a bench. Behind was an enclosed run for his chickens.

I cannot say that he was pleased to see us. He accepted our gifts as a right, without thanks, and grumbled a little because something or other he needed had not been brought. He was silent and morose. He was not interested in the news we had to give him, for the outside world was no concern of his: the only thing he cared about was his island. He looked upon it with a jealous, proprietary right; he called it "my health resort" and he feared that the coconuts that covered it would tempt some enterprising trader. He looked at me with suspicion. He was sombrely curious to know what I was doing in these seas. He used words with difficulty, talking to himself rather than to us, and it was a little uncanny to hear him mumble away as though we were not there. But he was moved when my skipper told him that an old man of his own age whom he had known for a long time was dead.

"Old Charlie dead—that's too bad. Old Charlie dead."

He repeated it over and over again. I asked him if he read.

"Not much," he answered indifferently.

He seemed to be occupied with nothing but his food, his dogs and his chickens. If what they tell us in books were true his long communion with nature and the sea should have taught him many subtle secrets. It hadn't. He was a savage. He was nothing but a narrow, ignorant and cantankerous seafaring man. As I looked at the wrinkled, mean old face I wondered what was the story of those three dreadful years that had made him welcome this long imprisonment. I sought to see behind those pale blue eyes of his what secrets they were that he would carry to his grave. And then I foresaw the end. One day a pearl fisher would land on the island and German Harry would not be waiting for him, silent and suspicious, at the water's edge. He would go up to the hut and there, lying on the bed, unrecognizable, he would see all that remained of what had once been a man. Perhaps then he would hunt high and low for the great mass of pearls that has haunted the fancy of so many adventurers. But I do not believe he would find it: German Harry would have seen to it that none should discover the treasure, and the pearls would rot in their hiding place. Then the pearl fisher would get back into his dinghy and the island once more be deserted of man.

# THE HAPPY MAN

It is a dangerous thing to order the lives of others and I have often wondered at the self-confidence of politicians, reformers and such like who are prepared to force upon their fellows measures that must alter their manners, habits and points of view. I have always hesitated to give advice, for how can one advise another how to act unless one knows that other as well as one knows oneself? Heavens knows, I know little enough of myself: I know nothing of others. We can only guess at the thoughts and emotions of our neighbours. Each one of us is a prisoner in a solitary tower and he communicates with the other prisoners, who form mankind, by conventional signs that have not quite the same meaning for them as for himself. And life, unfortunately, is something that you can lead but once; mistakes are often irreparable, and who am I that I should tell this one and that how he should lead it? Life is a difficult business and I have found it hard enough to make my own a complete and rounded thing; I have not been tempted to teach my neighbour what he should do with his. But there are men who flounder at the journey's start, the way before them is confused and hazardous, and on occasion, however unwillingly, I have been forced to point the finger of fate. Sometimes men have said to me, what shall I do with my life? and I have seen myself for a moment wrapped in the dark cloak of Destiny.

Once I know that I advised well.

I was a young man and I lived in a modest apartment in London near Victoria Station. Late one afternoon, when I was beginning to think that I had worked enough for that day, I heard a ring at the bell. I opened the door to a total stranger. He asked me my name; I told him. He asked if he might come in.

"Certainly."

I led him into my sitting-room and begged him to sit down. He seemed a trifle embarrassed. I offered him a cigarette and he had some difficulty in lighting it without letting go of his hat. When he had satisfactorily achieved this feat I asked him if I should not put it on a chair for him. He quickly did this and while doing it dropped his umbrella.

"I hope you don't mind my coming to see you like this," he said. "My name is Stephens and I am a doctor. You're in the medical, I believe?"

"Yes, but I don't practise."

"No, I know. I've just read a book of yours about Spain and I wanted to ask you about it."

"It's not a very good book, I'm afraid."

"The fact remains that you know something about Spain and there's no one else I know who does. And I thought perhaps you wouldn't mind giving me some information."

"I shall be very glad."

He was silent for a moment. He reached out for his hat and holding it in one hand absentmindedly stroked it with the other. I surmised that it gave him confidence.

"I hope you won't think it very odd for a perfect stranger to talk to you like this." He gave an apologetic laugh. "I'm not going to tell you the story of my life."

When people say this to me I always know that it is precisely what they are going to do. I do not mind. In fact I rather like it.

"I was brought up by two old aunts. I've never been anywhere. I've never done anything. I've been married for six years. I have no children. I'm medical officer at the Camberwell Infirmary. I can't stick it any more."

There was something very striking in the short, sharp sentences he used. They had a forcible ring. I had not given him more than a cursory glance, but now I looked at him with curiosity. He was a little man, thickset and stout, of thirty perhaps, with a round red face from which shone small, dark and very bright eyes. His black hair was cropped close to a bullet-shaped head. He was dressed in a blue suit a good deal the worse for wear. It was baggy at the knees and the pockets bulged untidily.

"You know what the duties are of a medical officer in an infirmary. One day is pretty much like another. And that's all I've got to look forward to for the rest of my life. Do you think it's worth it?"

"It's a means of livelihood," I answered.

"Yes, I know. The money's pretty good."

"I don't exactly know why you've come to me."

"Well, I wanted to know whether you thought there would be any chance for an English doctor in Spain?"

"Why Spain?"

"I don't know, I just have a fancy for it."

"It's not like Carmen, you know," I smiled.

"But there's sunshine there, and there's good wine, and there's colour, and there's air you can breathe. Let me say what I have to say straight out. I heard by accident that there was no English doctor in Seville. Do you think I could earn a living there? Is it madness to give up a good safe job for an uncertainty?"

"What does your wife think about it?"

"She's willing."

"It's a great risk."

"I know. But if you say take it, I will: if you say stay where you are, I'll stay."

He was looking at me intently with those bright dark eyes of his and I knew that he meant what he said. I reflected for a moment.

"Your whole future is concerned: you must decide for yourself. But this I can tell you: if you don't want money but are content to earn just enough to keep body and soul together, then go. For you will lead a wonderful life."

He left me, I thought about him for a day or two, and then forgot. The episode passed completely from my memory.

Many years later, fifteen at least, I happened to be in Seville and having some trifling indisposition asked the hotel porter whether there was an English doctor in the town. He said there was and gave me the address. I took a cab and as I drove up to the house a little fat man came out of it. He hesitated when he caught sight of me.

"Have you come to see me?" he said. "I'm the English doctor."

I explained my errand and he asked me to come in. He lived in an ordinary Spanish house, with a patio, and his consulting room which led out of it was littered with papers, books, medical appliances and lumber. The sight of it would have startled a squeamish patient. We did our business and then I asked the doctor what his fee was. He shook his head and smiled.

"There's no fee."

"Why on earth not?"

"Don't you remember me? Why, I'm here because of something you said to me. You changed my whole life for me. I'm Stephens."

I had not the least notion what he was talking about. He reminded me of our interview, he repeated to me what we had said, and gradually, out of the night, a dim recollection of the incident came back to me.

"I was wondering if I'd ever see you again," he said, "I was wondering if ever I'd have a chance of thanking you for all you've done for me."

"It's been a success then?"

I looked at him. He was very fat now and bald, but his eyes twinkled gaily and his fleshy, red face bore an expression of perfect good-humour. The clothes he wore, terribly shabby they were, had been made obviously by a Spanish tailor and his hat was the wide-brimmed sombrero of the Spaniard. He looked to me as though he knew a good bottle of wine when he saw it. He had a dissipated, though entirely sympathetic, appearance. You might have hesitated to let him remove your appendix, but you could not have imagined a more delightful creature to drink a glass of wine with.

"Surely you were married?" I said.

"Yes. My wife didn't like Spain, she went back to Camberwell, she was more at home there."

"Oh, I'm sorry for that."

His black eyes flashed a bacchanalian smile. He really had somewhat the look of a young Silenus.

"Life is full of compensations," he murmured.

The words were hardly out of his mouth when a Spanish woman, no longer in her first youth, but still boldly and voluptuously beautiful, appeared at the door. She spoke to him in Spanish, and I could not fail to perceive that she was the mistress of the house.

As he stood at the door to let me out he said to me:

"You told me when last I saw you that if I came here I should earn just enough money to keep body and soul together, but that I should lead a wonderful life. Well, I want to tell you that you were right. Poor I have been and poor I shall always be, but by heaven I've enjoyed myself. I wouldn't exchange the life I've had with that of any king in the world."

# THE DREAM

It chanced that in August, 1917, the work upon which I was then engaged obliged me to go from New York to Petrograd and I was instructed for safety's sake to travel by way of Vladivostok. I landed there in the morning and passed an idle day as best I could. The trans-Siberian train was due to start, so far as I remember, at about nine in the evening. I dined at the station restaurant by myself. It was crowded and I shared a small table with a man whose appearance entertained me. He was a Russian, a tall fellow, but amazingly stout, and he had so vast a paunch that he was obliged to sit well away from the table. His hands, small for his size, were buried in rolls of fat. His hair, long, dark and thin, was brushed carefully across his crown in order to conceal his baldness, and his huge sallow face, with its enormous double chin, clean-shaven, gave you an impression of indecent nakedness. His nose was small, a funny little button upon that mass of flesh, and his black shining eyes were small too. But he had a large, red and sensual mouth. He was dressed neatly enough in a black suit. It was not worn, but shabby; it looked as if it had been neither pressed nor brushed since he had had it.

The service was bad and it was almost impossible to attract the attention of a waiter. We soon got into conversation. The Russian spoke good and fluent English. His accent was marked but not tiresome. He asked me many questions about myself and my plans, which—my occupation at the time making caution necessary—I answered with a show of frankness but with dissimulation. I told him I was a journalist. He asked me whether I wrote fiction and when I confessed that in my leisure moments I did, he began to talk of the later Russian novelists. He spoke intelligently. It was plain that he was a man of education.

By this time we had persuaded the waiter to bring us some cabbage soup, and my acquaintance pulled a small bottle of vodka from his pocket which he invited me to share. I do not know whether it was the vodka or the natural loquaciousness of his race that made him communicative, but presently he told me, unasked, a good deal about himself. He was of noble birth, it appeared, a lawyer by profession, and a radical. Some trouble with the authorities had made it necessary for him to be much abroad, but now he was on his way home. Business had detained him at Vladivostok, but he expected to start for

Moscow in a week and if I went there he would be charmed to see me.

"Are you married?" he asked me.

I did not see what business it was of his, but I told him that I was. He sighed a little.

"I am a widower," he said. "My wife was a Swiss, a native of Geneva. She was a very cultivated woman. She spoke English, German and Italian perfectly. French, of course, was her native tongue. Her Russian was much above the average for a foreigner. She had scarcely the trace of an accent."

He called a waiter who was passing with a trayful of dishes and asked him, I suppose—for then I knew hardly any Russian—how much longer we were going to wait for the next course. The waiter, with a rapid but presumably reassuring exclamation, hurried on, and my friend sighed.

"Since the revolution the waiting in restaurants has become abominable."

He lighted his twentieth cigarette and I, looking at my watch, wondered whether I should get a square meal before it was time for me to start.

"My wife was a very remarkable woman," he continued. "She taught languages at one of the best schools for the daughters of noblemen in Petrograd. For a good many years we lived together on perfectly friendly terms. She was, however, of a jealous temperament and unfortunately she loved me to distraction."

It was difficult for me to keep a straight face. He was one of the ugliest men I had ever seen. There is sometimes a certain charm in the rubicund and jovial fat man, but this saturnine obesity was repulsive.

"I do not pretend that I was faithful to her. She was not young when I married her and we had been married for ten years. She was small and thin, and she had a bad complexion. She had a bitter tongue. She was a woman who suffered from a fury of possession, and she could not bear me to be attracted to anyone but her. She was jealous not only of the women I knew, but of my friends, my cat and my books. On one occasion in my absence she gave away a coat of mine merely because I liked none of my coats so well. But I am of an equable temperament. I will not deny that she bored me, but I accepted her acrimonious disposition as an act of God and no more thought of rebelling against it than I would against bad weather or a cold in the head. I denied her accusations as long as it was possible to deny them, and when it was impossible I shrugged my shoulders and smoked a cigarette.

"The constant scenes she made me did not very much affect me. I led my own life. Sometimes, indeed, I wondered whether it was passionate love she felt for me or passionate hate. It seemed to me that love and hate were very near allied.

"So we might have continued to the end of the chapter if one night a very curious thing had not happened. I was awakened by a piercing scream from my wife. Startled, I asked her what was the matter. She told me that she had had a fearful nightmare: she had dreamt that I was trying to kill her. We lived at the top of a large house and the well round which the stairs climbed was broad. She had dreamt that just as we had arrived at our own floor I had caught hold of her and attempted to throw her over the balusters. It was six stories to the stone floor at the bottom and it meant certain death.

"She was much shaken. I did my best to soothe her. But next morning, and for two or three days after, she referred to the subject again and, notwithstanding my laughter, I saw that it dwelt in her mind. I could not help thinking of it either, for this dream showed me something that I had never suspected. She thought I hated her, she thought I would gladly be rid of her; she knew of course that she was insufferable, and at some time or other the idea had evidently occurred to her that I was capable of murdering her. The thoughts of men are incalculable and ideas enter our minds that we should be ashamed to confess. Sometimes I had wished that she might run away with a lover, sometimes that a painless and sudden death might give me my freedom; but never, never had the idea come to me that I might deliberately rid myself of an intolerable burden.

"The dream made an extraordinary impression upon both of us. It frightened my wife, and she became for a little less bitter and more tolerant. But when I walked up the stairs to our apartment it was impossible for me not to look over the balusters and reflect how easy it would be to do what she had dreamt. The balusters were dangerously low. A quick gesture and the thing was done. It was hard to put the thought out of my mind. Then some months later my wife awakened me one night. I was very tired and I was exasperated. She was white and trembling. She had had the dream again. She burst into tears and asked me if I hated her. I swore by all the saints of the Russian calendar that I loved her. At last she went to sleep again. It was more than I could do. I lay awake. I seemed to see her falling down the well of the stairs, and I heard her shriek and the thud as she struck the stone floor. I could not help shivering."

The Russian stopped and beads of sweat stood

on his forehead. He had told the story well and fluently so that I had listened with attention. There was still some vodka in the bottle: he poured it out and swallowed it at a gulp.

"And how did your wife eventually die?" I asked after a pause.

He took out a dirty handkerchief and wiped his forehead.

"By an extraordinary coincidence she was found late one night at the bottom of the stairs with her neck broken."

"Who found her?"

"She was found by one of the lodgers who came in shortly after the catastrophe."

"And where were you?"

I cannot describe the look he gave me of malicious cunning. His little black eyes sparkled.

"I was spending the evening with a friend of mine. I did not come in till an hour later."

At that moment the waiter brought us the dish of meat that we had ordered, and the Russian fell upon it with good appetite. He shovelled the food into his mouth in enormous mouthfuls.

I was taken aback. Had he really been telling me in this hardly veiled manner that he had murdered his wife? That obese and sluggish man did not look like a murderer: I could not believe that he would have had the courage. Or was he making a sardonic joke at my expense?

In a few minutes it was time for me to go and catch my train. I left him and I have not seen him since. But I have never been able to make up my mind whether he was serious or jesting.

# IN A STRANGE LAND

I AM OF A ROVING DISPOSITION; but I travel not to see imposing monuments, which indeed somewhat bore me, nor beautiful scenery, of which I soon tire; I travel to see men. I avoid the great. I would not cross the road to meet a president or a king; I am content to know the writer in the pages of his book and the painter in his picture; but I have journeyed a hundred leagues to see a missionary of whom I had heard a strange story and I have spent a fortnight in a vile hotel in order to improve my acquaintance with a billiard marker. I should be inclined to say that I am not surprised to meet any sort of person were it not that there is one sort that I am constantly running against and that never fails to give me a little shock of amused astonishment. This is the elderly Englishwoman, generally of adequate means, who is to be found living alone, up and down the world, in unexpected places. You do not wonder when you hear of her living in a villa on a hill outside a small Italian town, the only Englishwoman in the neighbourhood, and you are almost prepared for it when a lonely hacienda is pointed out to you in Andalusia and you are told that there has dwelt for many years an English lady. But it is more surprising when you hear that the only white person in a Chinese city is an Englishwoman, not a missionary, who lives there none knows why; and there is another who inhabits an island in the South Seas and a third who has a bungalow on the outskirts of a large village in the centre of Java. They live solitary lives, these women, without friends, and they do not welcome the stranger. Though they may not have seen one of their own race for months they will pass you on the road as though they did not see you, and if, presuming on your nationality, you should call, as likely as not they will decline to see you; but if they do, they will give you a cup of tea from a silver teapot and on a plate of Old Worcester you will find Scotch scones. They will talk to you politely, as though they were entertaining you in a Kentish vicarage, but when you take your leave will show no particular desire to continue the acquaintance. One wonders in vain what strange instinct it is that has driven them to separate themselves from their kith and kin and thus to live apart from all their natural interests in an alien land. Is it romance they have sought or freedom?

But of all these Englishwomen whom I have met or perhaps only heard of (for as I have said they are difficult of access) the one who remains most vividly in my memory is an elderly person who lived in Asia Minor. I had arrived after a tedious journey at a little town from which I proposed to make the ascent of a celebrated mountain and I was taken to a rambling hotel that stood at its foot. I arrived late at night and signed my name in the book. I went up to my room. It was cold and I shivered as I undressed, but in a moment there was a knock at the door and the dragoman came in.

"Signora Niccolini's compliments," he said.

To my astonishment he handed me a hot-water bottle. I took it with grateful hands.

"Who is Signora Niccolini?" I asked.

"She is the proprietor of this hotel."

I sent her my thanks and he withdrew. The last thing I expected in a scrubby hotel in Asia Minor kept by an old Italian woman was a beautiful hot-water bottle. There is nothing I like more (if we were not all sick to death of the war I would tell you the story of how six men risked their lives to fetch a hot-water bottle from a château in Flanders that was being bombarded); and next morning, so that I might thank her in person, I asked if I might see the Signora Niccolini. While I waited for her I racked my brains to think what hot-water bottle could possibly be in Italian. In a moment she came in. She was a little stout woman, not without dignity, and she wore a black apron trimmed with lace and a small black lace cap. She stood with her hands crossed. I was astonished at her appearance for she looked exactly like a housekeeper in a great English house.

"Did you wish to speak to me, sir?"

She was an Englishwoman and in those few words I surely recognized the trace of a cockney accent.

"I wanted to thank you for the hot-water bottle," I replied in some confusion.

"I saw by the visitors' book that you were English, sir, and I always send up a 'ot-water bottle to English gentlemen."

"Believe me, it was very welcome."

"I was for many years in the service of the late Lord Ormskirk, sir. He always used to travel with a 'ot-water bottle. Is there anything else, sir?"

"Not at the moment, thank you."

She gave me a polite little nod and withdrew. I wondered how on earth it came about that a funny old Englishwoman like that should be the landlady of a hotel in Asia Minor. It was not easy to make her acquaintance, for she knew her place, as she would herself have put it, and she kept me at a distance. It was not for nothing that she had been in service in a noble English family. But I was persistent and I induced her at last to ask me to have a cup of tea in her own little parlour. I learnt that she had been lady's maid to a certain Lady Ormskirk, and Signor Niccolini (for she never alluded to her deceased husband in any other way) had been his lordship's chef. Signor Niccolini was a very handsome man and for some years there had been an "understanding" between them. When they had both saved a certain amount of money they were married, retired from service, and looked about for a hotel. They had bought this one on an advertisement because Signor Niccolini thought he would like to see something of the world. That was nearly thirty years ago and Signor Niccolini had been dead for fifteen. His widow had not once been back to England. I asked her if she was never homesick.

"I don't say as I wouldn't like to go back on a visit, though I expect I'd find many changes. But my family didn't like the idea of me marrying a foreigner and I 'aven't spoken to them since. Of course there are many things here that are not the same as what they 'ave at 'ome, but it's surprising what you get used to. I see a lot of life. I don't know as I should care to live the 'umdrum life they do in a place like London."

I smiled. For what she said was strangely incongruous with her manner. She was a pattern of decorum. It was extraordinary that she could have lived for thirty years in this wild, and almost barbaric, country without its having touched her. Though I knew no Turkish and she spoke it with ease I was convinced that she spoke it most incorrectly and with a cockney accent. I suppose she had remained the precise, prim English lady's maid, knowing her place, through all these vicissitudes because she had no faculty of surprise. She took everything that came as a matter of course. She looked upon everyone who wasn't English as a foreigner and therefore as someone, almost imbecile, for whom allowances must be made. She ruled her staff despotically—for did she not know how an upper servant in a great house should exercise his authority over the under servants?—and everything about the hotel was clean and neat.

"I do my best," she said, when I congratulated her on this, standing, as always when she spoke to me, with her hands respectfully crossed. "Of course one can't expect foreigners to 'ave the same ideas as we 'ave, but as his lordship used to say to me, what we've got to do, Parker, he said to me, what we've got to do in this life is to make the best of our raw material."

But she kept her greatest surprise for the eve of my departure.

"I'm glad you're not going before you've seen my two sons, sir."

"I didn't know you had any."

"They've been away on business, but they've just come back. You'll be surprised when you've seen them. I've trained them with me own 'ands so to speak, and when I'm gone they'll carry on the 'otel between them."

In a moment two tall, swarthy, strapping young fellows entered the hall. Her eyes lit up with pleasure. They went up to her and took her in their arms and gave her resounding kisses.

"They don't speak English, sir, but they understand a little, and of course they speak Turkish like natives, and Greek and Italian."

I shook hands with the pair and then Signora Niccolini said something to them and they went away.

"They're handsome fellows, signora," I said. "You must be very proud of them."

"I am, sir, and they're good boys, both of them. They've never give me a moment's trouble from the day they was born and they're the very image of Signor Niccolini."

"I must say no one would think they had an English mother."

"I'm not exactly their mother, sir. I've just sent them along to say 'ow do you do to 'er."

I dare say I looked a little confused.

"They're the sons that Signor Niccolini 'ad by a Greek girl that used to work in the 'otel, and 'aving no children of me own I adopted them."

I sought for some remark to make.

"I 'ope you don't think there's any blame attaches to Signor Niccolini," she said, drawing herself up a little. "I shouldn't like you to think that, sir." She folded her hands again and with a mixture of pride, primness and satisfaction added the final word: "Signor Niccolini was a very full-blooded man."

# THE LUNCHEON

I CAUGHT SIGHT of her at the play and in answer to her beckoning I went over during the interval and sat down beside her. It was long since I had last seen her and if someone had not mentioned her name I hardly think I would have recognized her. She addressed me brightly.

"Well, it's many years since we first met. How time does fly! We're none of us getting any younger. Do you remember the first time I saw you? You asked me to luncheon."

Did I remember?

It was twenty years ago and I was living in Paris. I had a tiny apartment in the Latin Quarter overlooking a cemetery and I was earning barely enough money to keep body and soul together. She had read a book of mine and had written to me about it. I answered, thanking her, and presently I received from her another letter saying that she was passing through Paris and would like to have a chat with me; but her time was limited and the only free moment she had was on the following Thursday; she was spending the morning at the Luxembourg and would I give her a little luncheon at Foyot's afterwards? Foyot's is a restaurant at which the French senators eat and it was so far beyond my means that I had never even thought of going there. But I was flattered and I was too young to have learned to say no to a woman. (Few men, I may add, learn this until they are too old to make it of any consequence to a woman what they say.) I had eighty francs (gold francs) to last me the rest of the month and a modest luncheon should not cost more than fifteen. If I cut out coffee for the next two weeks I could manage well enough.

I answered that I would meet my friend—by correspondence—at Foyot's on Thursday at half-past twelve. She was not so young as I expected and in appearance imposing rather than attractive. She was in fact a woman of forty (a charming age, but not one that excites a sudden and devastating passion at first sight), and she gave me the impression of having more teeth, white and large and even, than were necessary for any practical purpose. She was talkative, but since she seemed inclined to talk about me I was prepared to be an attentive listener.

I was startled when the bill of fare was brought, for the prices were a great deal higher than I had anticipated. But she reassured me.

"I never eat anything for luncheon," she said.

"Oh, don't say that!" I answered generously.

"I never eat more than one thing. I think people eat far too much nowadays. A little fish, perhaps. I wonder if they have any salmon."

Well, it was early in the year for salmon and it was not on the bill of fare, but I asked the waiter if there was any. Yes, a beautiful salmon had just come in, it was the first they had had. I ordered it for my guest. The waiter asked her if she would have something while it was being cooked.

"No," she answered, "I never eat more than one thing. Unless you had a little caviare. I never mind caviare."

My heart sank a little. I knew I could not afford caviare, but I could not very well tell her that. I told the waiter by all means to bring caviare. For myself I chose the cheapest dish on the menu and that was a mutton chop.

"I think you're unwise to eat meat," she said. "I don't know how you can expect to work after eating heavy things like chops. I don't believe in overloading my stomach."

Then came the question of drink.

"I never drink anything for luncheon," she said.

"Neither do I," I answered promptly.

"Except white wine," she proceeded as though I had not spoken. "These French white wines are so light. They're wonderful for the digestion."

"What would you like?" I asked, hospitable still, but not exactly effusive.

She gave me a bright and amicable flash of her white teeth.

"My doctor won't let me drink anything but champagne."

I fancy I turned a trifle pale. I ordered half a bottle. I mentioned casually that my doctor had absolutely forbidden me to drink champagne.

"What are you going to drink, then?"

"Water."

She ate the caviare and she ate the salmon. She talked gaily of art and literature and music. But I wondered what the bill would come to. When my mutton chop arrived she took me quite seriously to task.

"I see that you're in the habit of eating a heavy luncheon. I'm sure it's a mistake. Why don't you follow my example and just eat one thing? I'm sure you'd feel ever so much better for it."

"I *am* only going to eat one thing," I said, as the waiter came again with the bill of fare.

She waved him aside with an airy gesture.

"No, no, I never eat anything for luncheon. Just a bite, I never want more than that, and I eat that more as an excuse for conversation than anything else. I couldn't possibly eat anything more—unless they had some of those giant asparagus. I should be sorry to leave Paris without having some of them."

My heart sank. I had seen them in the shops and I knew that they were horribly expensive. My mouth had often watered at the sight of them.

"Madame wants to know if you have any of those giant asparagus," I asked the waiter.

I tried with all my might to will him to say no. A happy smile spread over his broad, priest-like face, and he assured me that they had some so large, so splendid, so tender, that it was a marvel.

"I'm not in the least hungry," my guest sighed, "but if you insist I don't mind having some asparagus."

I ordered them.

"Aren't you going to have any?"

"No, I never eat asparagus."

"I know there are people who don't like them. The fact is, you ruin your palate by all the meat you eat."

We waited for the asparagus to be cooked. Panic seized me. It was not a question now how much money I should have left over for the rest of the month, but whether I had enough to pay the bill. It would be mortifying to find myself ten francs short and be obliged to borrow from my guest. I could not bring myself to do that. I knew exactly how much I had and if the bill came to more I made up my mind that I would put my hand in my pocket and with a dramatic cry start up and say it had been picked. Of course it would be awkward if she had not money enough either to pay the bill. Then the only thing would be to leave my watch and say I would come back and pay later.

The asparagus appeared. They were enormous, succulent and appetizing. The smell of the melted butter tickled my nostrils as the nostrils of Jehovah were tickled by the burned offerings of the virtuous Semites. I watched the abandoned woman thrust them down her throat in large voluptuous mouthfuls and in my polite way I discoursed on the condition of the drama in the Balkans. At last she finished.

"Coffee?" I said.

"Yes, just an ice cream and coffee," she answered.

I was past caring now, so I ordered coffee for myself and an ice cream and coffee for her.

"You know, there's one thing I thoroughly believe in," she said, as she ate the ice cream. "One should always get up from a meal feeling one could eat a little more."

"Are you still hungry?" I asked faintly.

"Oh, no, I'm not hungry; you see, I don't eat luncheon. I have a cup of coffee in the morning and then dinner, but I never eat more than one thing for luncheon. I was speaking for you."

"Oh, I see!"

Then a terrible thing happened. While we were waiting for the coffee, the head waiter, with an ingratiating smile on his false face, came up to us bearing a large basket full of huge peaches. They had the blush of an innocent girl; they had the rich tone of an Italian landscape. But surely peaches were not in season then? Lord knew what they cost. I knew too—a little later, for my guest, going on with her conversation, absent-mindedly took one.

"You see, you've filled your stomach with a lot of meat"—my one miserable little chop—"and you can't eat any more. But I've just had a snack and I shall enjoy a peach."

The bill came and when I paid it I found that I had only enough for a quite inadequate tip. Her eyes rested for an instant on the three francs I left for the waiter and I knew that she thought me mean. But when I walked out of the restaurant I had the whole month before me and not a penny in my pocket.

"Follow my example," she said as we shook hands, "and never eat more than one thing for luncheon."

"I'll do better than that," I retorted. "I'll eat nothing for dinner tonight."

"Humorist!" she cried gaily, jumping into a cab. "You're quite a humorist!"

But I have had my revenge at last. I do not believe that I am a vindictive man, but when the immortal gods take a hand in the matter it is pardonable to observe the result with complacency. Today she weighs three hundred pounds.

# SALVATORE

I WONDER if I can do it.

I knew Salvatore first when he was a boy of fifteen with a pleasant, ugly face, a laughing mouth and carefree eyes. He used to spend the morning lying about the beach with next to nothing on and his brown body was as thin as a rail. He was full of grace. He was in and out of the sea all the time, swimming with the clumsy, effortless stroke common to the fisher boys. Scrambling up the jagged rocks on his hard feet, for except on Sundays he never wore shoes, he would throw himself into the deep water with a cry of delight. His father was a fisherman who owned his own little vineyard and Salvatore acted as nursemaid to his two younger brothers. He shouted to them to come in shore when they ventured out too far and made them dress when it was time to climb the hot vine-clad hill for the frugal midday meal.

But boys in those Southern parts grow apace and in a little while he was madly in love with a pretty girl who lived on the Grande Marina. She had eyes like forest pools and held herself like a daughter of the Caesars. They were affianced, but they could not marry till Salvatore had done his military service, and when he left the island which he had never left in his life before, to become a sailor in the navy of King Victor Emmanuel, he wept like a child. It was hard for one who had never been less free than the birds to be at the beck and call of others; it was harder still to live in a battleship with strangers instead of in a little white cottage among the vines; and when he was ashore, to walk in noisy, friendless cities with streets so crowded that he was frightened to cross them, when he had been used to silent paths and the mountains and the sea. I suppose it had never struck him that Ischia, which he looked at every evening (it was like a fairy island in the sunset) to see what the weather would be like next day, or Vesuvius, pearly in the dawn, had anything to do with him at all; but when he ceased to have them before his eyes he realized in some dim fashion that they were as much part of him as his hands and his feet. He was dreadfully homesick. But it was hardest of all to be parted from the girl he loved with all his passionate young heart. He wrote to her (in his childlike handwriting) long, ill-spelt letters in which he told her how constantly he thought of her and how much he longed to be back. He was sent here and there, to Spezzia, to Venice, to Bari and finally to China. Here he fell ill of some mysterious ailment that kept him in hospital for months. He bore it with the mute and uncomprehending patience of a dog. When he learnt that it was a form of rheumatism that made him unfit for further service his heart exulted, for he could go home; and he did not bother, in fact he scarcely listened, when the doctors told him that he would never again be quite well. What did he care when he was going back to the little island he loved so well and the girl who was waiting for him?

When he got into the rowing-boat that met the steamer from Naples and was rowed ashore he saw his father and mother standing on the jetty and his two brothers, big boys now, and he waved to them. His eyes searched among the crowd that waited there for the girl. He could not see her. There was a great deal of kissing when he jumped up the steps and they all, emotional creatures, cried a little as they exchanged their greetings. He asked where the girl was. His mother told him that she did not know; they had not seen her for two or three weeks; so in the evening when the moon was shining over the placid sea and the lights of Naples twinkled in the distance he walked down to the Grande Marina to her house. She was sitting on the doorstep with her mother. He was a little shy because he had not seen her for so long. He asked her if she had not received the letter that he had written to her to say that he was coming home. Yes, they had received a letter, and they had been told by another of the island boys that he was ill. Yes, that was why he was back; was it not a piece of luck? Oh, but they had heard that he would never be quite well again. The doctors talked a lot of nonsense, but he knew very well that now he was home again he would recover. They were silent for a little, and then the mother nudged the girl. She did not try to soften the blow. She told him straight out, with the blunt directness of her race, that she could not marry a man who would never be strong enough to work like a man. They had made up their minds, her mother and father and she, and her father would never give his consent.

When Salvatore went home he found that they all knew. The girl's father had been to tell them what they had decided, but they had lacked the courage to tell him themselves. He wept on his mother's bosom. He was terribly unhappy, but he did not blame the girl. A fisherman's life is hard and it needs strength and endurance. He knew very well that a girl could not afford to marry a man who might not be able to support her. His smile was very sad and his eyes had the look of a dog that has been beaten, but he did not complain, and he never said a hard word of the girl he had loved so well. Then, a few months later, when he had settled down to the common round, working in his father's vineyard and fishing, his mother told him that there was a young woman in the village who was willing to marry him. Her name was Assunta.

"She's as ugly as the devil," he said.

She was older than he, twenty-four or twenty-five, and she had been engaged to a man who, while doing his military service, had been killed in Africa. She had a little money of her own and if Salvatore married her she could buy him a boat of his own and they could take a vineyard that by a happy chance happened at that moment to be without a tenant. His mother told him that Assunta had seen him at the festa and had fallen in love with him. Salvatore smiled his sweet smile and said he would think about it. On the following Sunday, dressed in the stiff black clothes in which he looked so much less well than in the ragged shirt and trousers of every day, he went up to High Mass at the parish church and placed himself so that he could have a good look at the young woman. When he came down again he told his mother that he was willing.

Well, they were married and they settled down in a tiny whitewashed house in the middle of a handsome vineyard. Salvatore was now a great big husky fellow, tall and broad, but still with that ingenuous smile and those trusting, kindly eyes that he had had as a boy. He had the most beautiful manners I have ever seen in my life. Assunta was a grim-visaged female, with decided features, and she looked old for her years. But she had a good heart and she was no fool. I used to be amused by the little smile of devotion that she gave her husband when he was being very masculine and masterful; she never ceased to be touched by his gentle sweetness. But she could not bear the girl who had thrown him over, and notwithstanding Salvatore's smiling expostulations she had nothing but harsh words for her. Presently children were born to them.

It was a hard enough life. All through the fishing season towards evening he set out in his boat with one of his brothers for the fishing grounds. It was a long pull of six or seven miles and he spent the night catching the profitable cuttlefish. Then there was the long row back again in order to sell the catch in time for it to go on the early boat to Naples. At other times he was working in his vineyard from dawn till the heat drove him to rest and then again, when it was a trifle cooler, till dusk. Often his rheumatism prevented him from doing anything at all and then he would lie about the beach, smoking cigarettes, with a pleasant word for everyone notwithstanding the pain that racked his limbs. The foreigners who came down to bathe and saw him there said that these Italian fishermen were lazy devils.

Sometimes he used to bring his children down to give them a bath. They were both boys and at this time the elder was three and the younger less than two. They sprawled about at the water's edge stark naked and Salvatore, standing on a rock, would dip them in the water. The elder one bore it with stoicism, but the baby screamed lustily. Salvatore had enormous hands, like legs of mutton, coarse and hard from constant toil, but when he bathed his children, holding them so tenderly, drying them with delicate care, upon my word they were like flowers. He would seat the naked baby on the palm of his hand and hold him up, laughing a little at his smallness, and his laugh was like the laughter of an angel. His eyes then were as candid as his child's.

I started by saying that I wondered if I could do it and now I must tell you what it is that I have tried to do. I wanted to see whether I could hold your attention for a few pages while I drew for you the portrait of a man, just an ordinary Italian fisherman who possessed nothing in the world except a quality which is the rarest, the most precious and the loveliest that anyone can have. Heaven only knows why he should so strangely and unexpectedly have possessed it. All I know is that it shone in him with a radiance that, if it had not been so unconscious and so humble, would have been to the common run of men hardly bearable. And in case you have not guessed what the quality was I will tell you. Goodness, just goodness.

# HOME

THE FARM LAY in a hollow among the Somersetshire hills, an old-fashioned stone house surrounded by barns and pens and outhouses. Over the doorway the date when it was built had been carved in the elegant figures of the period, 1673, and the house, gray and weather-beaten, looked as much a part of the landscape as the trees that sheltered it. An avenue of splendid elms that would have been the pride of many a squire's mansion led from the road to the trim garden. The people who lived here were as stolid, sturdy and unpretentious as the house; their only boast was that ever since it was built from father to son in one unbroken line they had been born and died in it. For three hundred years they had farmed the surrounding land. George Meadows was now a man of fifty, and his wife was a year or two younger. They were both fine, upstanding people in the prime of life; and their children, two sons and three girls, were handsome and strong. They had no newfangled notions about being gentlemen and ladies; they knew their place and were proud of it. I have never seen a more united household. They were merry, industrious and kindly.

Their life was patriarchal. It had a completeness that gave it a beauty as definite as that of a symphony by Beethoven or a picture by Titian. They were happy and they deserved their happiness. But the master of the house was not George Meadows (not by a long chalk, they said in the village): it was his mother. She was twice the man her son was, they said. She was a woman of seventy, tall, upright and dignified, with gray hair, and though her face was much wrinkled, her eyes were bright and shrewd. Her word was law in the house and on the farm; but she had humour, and if her rule was despotic it was also kindly. People laughed at her jokes and repeated them. She was a good business woman and you had to get up very early in the morning to best her in a bargain. She was a character. She combined in a rare degree good will with an alert sense of the ridiculous.

One day Mrs George stopped me on my way home. She was all in a flutter. (Her mother-in-law was the only Mrs Meadows we knew: George's wife was known only as Mrs George.)

"Whoever do you think is coming here today?" she asked me. "Uncle George Meadows. You know, him as was in China."

"Why, I thought he was dead."

"We all thought he was dead."

I had heard the story of Uncle George Meadows a dozen times and it had amused me because it had the savour of an old ballad: it was oddly touching to come across it in real life. For Uncle George Meadows and Tom, his younger brother, had both courted Mrs Meadows when she was Emily Green, fifty years and more ago, and when she married Tom, George had gone away to sea.

They heard of him on the China coast. For twenty years now and then he sent them presents; then there was no more news of him; when Tom Meadows died his widow wrote and told him, but received no answer; and at last they came to the conclusion that he must be dead. But two or three days ago to their astonishment they had received a letter from the matron of the sailors' home at Portsmouth. It appeared that for the last ten years George Meadows, crippled with rheumatism, had been an inmate and now, feeling that he had not much longer to live, wanted to see once more the house in which he was born. Albert Meadows, his great-nephew, had gone over to Portsmouth in the Ford to fetch him and he was to arrive that afternoon.

"Just fancy," said Mrs George, "he's not been here for more than fifty years. He's never even seen my George who's fifty-one next birthday."

"And what does Mrs Meadows think of it?" I asked.

"Well, you know what she is. She sits there and smiles to herself. All she says is, 'He was a good-looking young fellow when he left, but not so steady as his brother.' That's why she chose my George's father. 'But he's probably quietened down by now,' she says."

Mrs George asked me to look in and see him. With the simplicity of a countrywoman who had never been further from her home than London, she thought that because we had both been in China we must have something in common. Of course I accepted. I found the whole family assembled when I arrived; they were sitting in the great old kitchen, with its stone floor, Mrs Meadows in her usual chair by the fire, very upright, and I was amused to see that she had put on her best silk dress, while her son and his wife sat at the table with their children. On the other side of the fireplace sat an old man, bunched up in a chair. He was very thin and his skin hung on his bones like an old suit much too large for him; his face was wrinkled and yellow and he had lost nearly all his teeth.

I shook hands with him.

"Well, I'm glad to see you've got here safely, Mr Meadows," I said.

"Captain," he corrected.

"He walked here," Albert, his great-nephew, told me. "When he got to the gate he made me stop the car and said he wanted to walk."

"And mind you, I've not been out of me bed for two years. They carried me down and put me in the car. I thought I'd never walk again, but when I see them elm trees, I remember my father set a lot of store by them elm trees, I felt I could walk. I walked down that drive fifty-two years ago when I went away and now I've walked back again."

"Silly, I call it," said Mrs Meadows.

"It's done me good. I feel better and stronger than I have for ten years. I'll see you out yet, Emily."

"Don't you be too sure," she answered.

I suppose no one had called Mrs Meadows by her first name for a generation. It gave me a little shock, as though the old man were taking a liberty with her. She looked at him with a shrewd smile in her eyes and he, talking to her, grinned with his toothless gums. It was strange to look at them, these two old people who had not seen one another for half a century, and to think that all that long time ago he had loved her and she had loved another. I wondered if they remembered what they had felt then and what they had said to one another.

I wondered if it seemed to him strange now that for that old woman he had left the home of his fathers, his lawful inheritance, and lived an exile's life.

"Have you ever been married, Captain Meadows?" I asked.

"Not me," he said, in his quavering voice, with a grin. "I know too much about women for that."

"That's what you say," retorted Mrs Meadows. "If the truth was known I shouldn't be surprised to hear as how you'd had half-a-dozen black wives in your day."

"They're not black in China, Emily, you ought to know better than that, they're yellow."

"Perhaps that's why you've got so yellow yourself. When I saw you, I said to myself, why, he's got jaundice."

"I said I'd never marry anyone but you, Emily, and I never have."

He said this not with pathos or resentment, but as a mere statement of fact, as a man might say, I said I'd walk twenty miles and I've done it. There was a trace of satisfaction in the speech.

"Well, you might have regretted it if you had," she answered.

I talked a little with the old man about China.

"There's not a port in China that I don't know better than you know your coat pocket. Where a ship can go I've been. I could keep you sitting here all day long for six months and not tell you half the things I've seen in my day."

"Well, one thing you've not done, George, as far as I can see," said Mrs Meadows, the mocking but not unkindly smile still in her eyes, "and that's to make a fortune."

"I'm not one to save money. Make it and spend it: that's my motto. But one thing I can say for myself: if I had the chance of going through my life again I'd take it. And there's not many as'll say that."

"No, indeed," I said.

I looked at him with admiration and respect. He was a toothless, crippled, penniless old man, but he had made a success of life, for he had enjoyed it. When I left him he asked me to come and see him again next day. If I was interested in China he would tell me all the stories I wanted to hear.

Next morning I thought I would go and ask if the old man would like to see me. I strolled down the magnificent avenue of elm trees and when I came to the garden saw Mrs Meadows picking flowers. I bade her good morning and she raised herself. She had a huge armful of white flowers. I glanced at the house and saw that the blinds were drawn: I was surprised, for Mrs Meadows liked the sunshine.

"Time enough to live in the dark when you're buried," she always said.

"How's Captain Meadows?" I asked her.

"He always was a harum-scarum fellow," she answered. "When Lizzie took him in a cup of tea this morning she found he was dead."

"Dead?"

"Yes. Died in his sleep. I was just picking these flowers to put in the room. Well, I'm glad he died in that old house. It always means a lot to them Meadows to do that."

They had had a good deal of difficulty in persuading him to go to bed. He had talked to them of all the things that had happened to him in his long life. He was happy to be back in his old home. He was proud that he had walked up the drive without assistance, and he boasted that he would live for another twenty years. But fate had been kind: death had written the full stop in the right place.

Mrs Meadows smelt the white flowers that she held in her arms.

"Well, I'm glad he came back," she said. "After I married Tom Meadows and George went away, the fact is I was never quite sure that I'd married the right one."

# MR KNOW-ALL

I WAS PREPARED to dislike Max Kelada even before I knew him. The war had just finished and the passenger traffic in the ocean-going liners was heavy. Accommodation was very hard to get and you had to put up with whatever the agents chose to offer you. You could not hope for a cabin to yourself and I was thankful to be given one in which there were only two berths. But when I was told the name of my companion my heart sank. It suggested closed portholes and the night air rigidly excluded. It was bad enough to share a cabin for fourteen days with anyone (I was going from San Francisco to Yokohama), but I should have looked upon it with less dismay if my fellow passenger's name had been Smith or Brown.

When I went on board I found Mr Kelada's luggage already below. I did not like the look of it; there were too many labels on the suitcases, and the wardrobe trunk was too big. He had unpacked his toilet things, and I observed that he was a patron of the excellent Monsieur Coty; for I saw on the washing-stand his scent, his hairwash and his brilliantine. Mr Kelada's brushes, ebony with his monogram in gold, would have been all the better for a scrub. I did not at all like Mr Kelada. I made my way into the smoking-room. I called for a pack of cards and began to play patience. I had scarcely started before a man came up to me and asked me if he was right in thinking my name was so and so.

"I am Mr Kelada," he added, with a smile that showed a row of flashing teeth, and sat down.

"Oh, yes, we're sharing a cabin, I think."

"Bit of luck, I call it. You never know who you're going to be put in with. I was jolly glad when I heard you were English. I'm all for us English sticking together when we're abroad, if you understand what I mean."

I blinked.

"Are you English?" I asked, perhaps tactlessly.

"Rather. You don't think I look like an American, do you? British to the backbone, that's what I am."

To prove it, Mr Kelada took out of his pocket a passport and airily waved it under my nose.

King George has many strange subjects. Mr Kelada was short and of a sturdy build, clean-shaven and dark skinned, with a fleshy, hooked nose and very large, lustrous and liquid eyes. His long black hair was sleek and curly. He spoke with a fluency in which there was nothing English and his gestures were exuberant. I felt pretty sure that a closer inspection of that British passport would have betrayed the fact that Mr Kelada was born under a bluer sky than is generally seen in England.

"What will you have?" he asked me.

I looked at him doubtfully. Prohibition was in force and to all appearance the ship was bone dry. When I am not thirsty I do not know which I dislike more, ginger ale or lemon squash. But Mr Kelada flashed an oriental smile at me.

"Whisky and soda or a dry martini, you have only to say the word."

From each of his hip pockets he fished a flask and laid it on the table before me. I chose the martini, and calling the steward he ordered a tumbler of ice and a couple of glasses.

"A very good cocktail," I said.

"Well, there are plenty more where that came from, and if you've got any friends on board, you tell them you've got a pal who's got all the liquor in the world."

Mr Kelada was chatty. He talked of New York and of San Francisco. He discussed plays, pictures, and politics. He was patriotic. The Union Jack is an impressive piece of drapery, but when it is flourished by a gentleman from Alexandria or Beirut, I cannot but feel that it loses somewhat in dignity. Mr Kelada was familiar. I do not wish to put on airs, but I cannot help feeling that it is seemly in a total stranger to put mister before my name when he addresses me. Mr Kelada, doubtless to set me at my ease, used no such formality. I did not like Mr Kelada. I had put aside the cards when he sat down, but now, thinking that for this first occasion our conversation had lasted long enough, I went on with my game.

"The three on the four," said Mr Kelada.

There is nothing more exasperating when you are playing patience than to be told where to put the card you have turned up before you have had a chance to look for yourself.

"It's coming out, it's coming out," he cried. "The ten on the knave."

With rage and hatred in my heart I finished. Then he seized the pack.

"Do you like card tricks?"

"No, I hate card tricks," I answered.

"Well, I'll just show you this one."

He showed me three. Then I said I would go down to the dining-room and get my seat at table.

"Oh, that's all right," he said. "I've already taken a seat for you. I thought that as we were in the same stateroom we might just as well sit at the same table."

I did not like Mr Kelada.

I not only shared a cabin with him and ate three meals a day at the same table, but I could not walk round the deck without his joining me. It was impossible to snub him. It never occurred to him that he was not wanted. He was certain that you were as glad to see him as he was to see you. In your own house you might have kicked him downstairs and slammed the door in his face without the suspicion dawning on him that he was not a welcome visitor. He was a good mixer, and in three days knew everyone on board. He ran everything. He managed the sweeps, conducted the auctions, collected money for prizes at the sports, got up quoit and golf matches, organized the concert and arranged the fancy-dress ball. He was everywhere and always. He was certainly the best hated man in the ship. We called him Mr Know-All, even to his face. He took it as a compliment. But it was at mealtimes that he was most intolerable. For the better part of an hour then he had us at his mercy. He was hearty, jovial, loquacious and argumentative. He knew everything better than anybody else, and it was an affront to his overweening vanity that you should disagree with him. He would not drop a subject, however unimportant, till he had brought you round to his way of thinking. The possibility that he could be mistaken never occurred to him. He was the chap who knew. We sat at the doctor's table. Mr Kelada would certainly have had it all his own way, for the doctor was lazy and I was frigidly indifferent, except for a man called Ramsay who sat there also. He was as dogmatic as Mr Kelada and resented bitterly the Levantine's cocksureness. The discussions they had were acrimonious and interminable.

Ramsay was in the American Consular Service and was stationed at Kobe. He was a great heavy fellow from the Middle West, with loose fat under a tight skin, and he bulged out of his ready-made clothes. He was on his way back to resume his post, having been on a flying visit to New York to fetch his wife who had been spending a year at home. Mrs Ramsay was a very pretty little thing, with pleasant manners and a sense of humour. The Consular Service is ill paid, and she was dressed always very simply; but she knew how to wear her clothes. She achieved an effect of quiet distinction. I should not have paid any particular attention to her but that she possessed a quality that may be common enough in women, but nowadays is not obvious in their demeanour. You could not look at her without being struck by her modesty. It shone in her like a flower on a coat.

One evening at dinner the conversation by chance drifted to the subject of pearls. There had been in the papers a good deal of talk about the culture pearls which the cunning Japanese were making, and the doctor remarked that they must inevitably diminish the value of real ones. They were very good already; they would soon be perfect. Mr Kelada, as was his habit, rushed the new topic. He told us all that was to be known about pearls. I do not believe Ramsay knew anything about them at all, but he could not resist the opportunity to have a fling at the Levantine, and in five minutes we were in the middle of a heated argument. I had seen Mr Kelada vehement and voluble before, but never so voluble and vehement as now. At last something that Ramsay said stung him, for he thumped the table and shouted:

"Well, I ought to know what I am talking about. I'm going to Japan just to look into this Japanese pearl business. I'm in the trade and there's not a man in it who won't tell you that what I say about pearls goes. I know all the best pearls in the world, and what I don't know about pearls isn't worth knowing."

Here was news for us, for Mr Kelada, with all his loquacity, had never told anyone what his business was. We only knew vaguely that he was going to Japan on some commercial errand. He looked round the table triumphantly.

"They'll never be able to get a culture pearl that an expert like me can't tell with half an eye." He pointed to a chain that Mrs Ramsay wore. "You take my word for it, Mrs Ramsay, that chain you're wearing will never be worth a cent less than it is now."

Mrs Ramsay in her modest way flushed a little and slipped the chain inside her dress. Ramsay leaned forward. He gave us all a look and a smile flickered in his eyes.

"That's a pretty chain of Mrs Ramsay's, isn't it?"

"I noticed it at once," answered Mr Kelada. "Gee, I said to myself, those are pearls all right."

"I didn't buy it myself, of course. I'd be interested to know how much you think it cost."

"Oh, in the trade somewhere round fifteen thousand dollars. But if it was bought on Fifth Avenue I shouldn't be surprised to hear that anything up to thirty thousand was paid for it."

Ramsay smiled grimly.

"You'll be surprised to hear that Mrs Ramsay bought that string at a department store the day before we left New York, for eighteen dollars."

Mr Kelada flushed.

"Rot. It's not only real, but it's as fine a string for its size as I've ever seen."

"Will you bet on it? I'll bet you a hundred dollars it's imitation."

"Done."

"Oh, Elmer, you can't bet on a certainty," said Mrs Ramsay.

She had a little smile on her lips and her tone was gently deprecating.

"Can't I? If I get a chance of easy money like that I should be all sorts of a fool not to take it."

"But how can it be proved?" she continued. "It's only my word against Mr Kelada's."

"Let me look at the chain, and if it's imitation I'll tell you quickly enough. I can afford to lose a hundred dollars," said Mr Kelada.

"Take it off, dear. Let the gentleman look at it as much as he wants."

Mrs Ramsay hesitated a moment. She put her hands to the clasp.

"I can't undo it," she said. "Mr Kelada will just have to take my word for it."

I had a sudden suspicion that something unfortunate was about to occur, but I could think of nothing to say.

Ramsay jumped up.

"I'll undo it."

He handed the chain to Mr Kelada. The Levantine took a magnifying glass from his pocket and closely examined it. A smile of triumph spread over his smooth and swarthy face. He handed back the chain. He was about to speak. Suddenly he caught sight of Mrs Ramsay's face. It was so white that she looked as though she were about to faint. She was staring at him with wide and terrified eyes. They held a desperate appeal; it was so clear that I wondered why her husband did not see it.

Mr Kelada stopped with his mouth open. He flushed deeply. You could almost *see* the effort he was making over himself.

"I was mistaken," he said. "It's a very good imitation, but of course as soon as I looked through my glass I saw that it wasn't real. I think eighteen dollars is just about as much as the damned thing's worth."

He took out his pocketbook and from it a hundred-dollar bill. He handed it to Ramsay without a word.

"Perhaps that'll teach you not to be so cocksure another time, my young friend," said Ramsay as he took the note.

I noticed that Mr Kelada's hands were trembling.

The story spread over the ship as stories do, and he had to put up with a good deal of chaff that evening. It was a fine joke that Mr Know-All had been caught out. But Mrs Ramsay retired to her stateroom with a headache.

Next morning I got up and began to shave. Mr Kelada lay on his bed smoking a cigarette. Suddenly there was a small scraping sound and I saw a letter pushed under the door. I opened the door and looked out. There was nobody there. I picked up the letter and saw that it was addressed to Max Kelada. The name was written in block letters. I handed it to him.

"Who's this from?" He opened it. "Oh!"

He took out of the envelope, not a letter, but a hundred-dollar bill. He looked at me and again he reddened. He tore the envelope into little bits and gave them to me.

"Do you mind just throwing them out of the porthole?"

I did as he asked, and then I looked at him with a smile.

"No one likes being made to look a perfect damned fool," he said.

"Were the pearls real?"

"If I had a pretty little wife I shouldn't let her spend a year in New York while I stayed at Kobe," said he.

At that moment I did not entirely dislike Mr Kelada. He reached out for his pocketbook and carefully put in it the hundred-dollar note.

# THE ESCAPE

I HAVE ALWAYS BEEN CONVINCED that if a woman once made up her mind to marry a man nothing but instant flight could save him. Not always that; for once a friend of mine, seeing the inevitable loom menacingly before him, took ship from a certain port (with a toothbrush for all his luggage, so conscious was he of his danger and the necessity for immediate action) and spent a year travelling round the world; but when, thinking himself safe (women are fickle, he said, and in twelve months she will have forgotten all about me), he landed at the self-same port the first person he saw gaily waving to him from the quay was the little lady from whom he had fled. I have only once known a man who in such circumstances managed to extricate himself. His name was Roger Charing. He was no longer young when he fell in love with Ruth Barlow and he had had sufficient experience to make him careful; but Ruth Barlow had a gift (or should I call it a quality?) that renders most men defenceless, and it was this that dispossessed Roger of his common sense, his prudence and his worldly wisdom. He went down like a row of ninepins. This was the gift of pathos.

Mrs Barlow, for she was twice a widow, had splendid dark eyes and they were the most moving I ever saw; they seemed to be ever on the point of filling with tears; they suggested that the world was too much for her, and you felt that, poor dear, her sufferings had been more than anyone should be asked to bear. If, like Roger Charing, you were a strong, hefty fellow with plenty of money, it was almost inevitable that you should say to yourself: I must stand between the hazards of life and this helpless little thing, oh, how wonderful it would be to take the sadness out of those big and lovely eyes! I gathered from Roger that everyone had treated Mrs Barlow very badly. She was apparently one of those unfortunate persons with whom nothing by any chance goes right. If she married a husband he beat her; if she employed a broker he cheated her; if she engaged a cook she drank. She never had a little lamb but it was sure to die.

When Roger told me that he had at last persuaded her to marry him, I wished him joy.

"I hope you'll be good friends," he said. "She's a little afraid of you, you know; she thinks you're callous."

"Upon my word I don't know why she should think that."

"You do like her, don't you?"

"Very much."

"She's had a rotten time, poor dear. I feel so dreadfully sorry for her."

"Yes," I said.

I couldn't say less. I knew she was stupid and I thought she was scheming. My own belief was that she was as hard as nails.

The first time I met her we had played bridge together and when she was my partner she twice trumped my best card. I behaved like an angel, but I confess that I thought if the tears were going to well up into anybody's eyes they should have been mine rather than hers. And when, having by the end of the evening lost a good deal of money to me, she said she would send me a cheque and never did, I could not but think that I and not she should have worn a pathetic expression when next we met.

Roger introduced her to his friends. He gave her jewels. He took her here, there, and everywhere. Their marriage was announced for the immediate future. Roger was very happy. He was committing a good action and at the same time doing something he had very much a mind to. It is an uncommon situation and it is not surprising if he was a trifle more pleased with himself than was altogether becoming.

Then, on a sudden, he fell out of love. I do not

know why. It could hardly have been that he grew tired of her conversation, for she had never had any conversation. Perhaps it was merely that this pathetic look of hers ceased to wring his heart-strings. His eyes were opened and he was once more the shrewd man of the world he had been. He became acutely conscious that Ruth Barlow had made up her mind to marry him and he swore a solemn oath that nothing would induce him to marry Ruth Barlow. But he was in a quandary. Now that he was in possession of his senses he saw with clearness the sort of woman he had to deal with and he was aware that, if he asked her to release him, she would (in her appealing way) assess her wounded feelings at an immoderately high figure. Besides, it is always awkward for a man to jilt a woman. People are apt to think he has behaved badly.

Roger kept his own counsel. He gave neither by word nor gesture an indication that his feelings towards Ruth Barlow had changed. He remained attentive to all her wishes; he took her to dine at restaurants, they went to the play together, he sent her flowers; he was sympathetic and charming. They had made up their minds that they would be married as soon as they found a house that suited them, for he lived in chambers and she in furnished rooms; and they set about looking at desirable residences.

The agents sent Roger orders to view and he took Ruth to see a number of houses. It was very hard to find anything that was quite satisfactory. Roger applied to more agents. They visited house after house. They went over them thoroughly, examining them from the cellars in the basement to the attics under the roof. Sometimes they were too large and sometimes they were too small; sometimes they were too far from the centre of things and sometimes they were too close; sometimes they were too expensive and sometimes they wanted too many repairs; sometimes they were too stuffy and sometimes they were too airy; sometimes they were too dark and sometimes they were too bleak. Roger always found a fault that made the house unsuitable. Of course he was hard to please; he could not bear to ask his dear Ruth to live in any but the perfect house, and the perfect house wanted finding. Househunting is a tiring and a tiresome business and presently Ruth began to grow peevish. Roger begged her to have patience; somewhere, surely, existed the very house they were looking for, and it only needed a little perseverance and they would find it. They looked at hundreds of houses; they climbed thousands of stairs; they inspected innumerable kitchens. Ruth was exhausted and more than once lost her temper.

"If you don't find a house soon," she said, "I shall

have to reconsider my position. Why, if you go on like this we shan't be married for years."

"Don't say that," he answered, "I beseech you to have patience. I've just received some entirely new lists from agents I've only just heard of. There must be at least sixty houses on them."

They set out on the chase again. They looked at more houses and more houses. For two years they looked at houses. Ruth grew silent and scornful: her pathetic, beautiful eyes acquired an expression that was almost sullen. There are limits to human endurance. Mrs Barlow had the patience of an angel, but at last she revolted.

"Do you want to marry me or do you not?" she asked him.

There was an unaccustomed hardness in her voice, but it did not affect the gentleness of his reply.

"Of course I do. We'll be married the very moment we find a house. By the way I've just heard of something that might suit us."

"I don't feel well enough to look at any more houses just yet."

"Poor dear, I was afraid you were looking rather tired."

Ruth Barlow took to her bed. She would not see Roger and he had to content himself with calling at her lodgings to inquire and sending her flowers. He was as ever assiduous and gallant. Every day he wrote and told her that he had heard of another house for them to look at. A week passed and then he received the following letter:

ROGER:

*I do not think you really love me. I have found someone who is anxious to take care of me and I am going to be married to him today.*

RUTH.

He sent back his reply by special messenger.

RUTH:

*Your news shatters me. I shall never get over the blow, but of course your happiness must be my first consideration. I send you herewith seven orders to view; they arrived by this morning's post and I am quite sure you will find among them a house that will exactly suit you.*

ROGER.

# A FRIEND IN NEED

FOR THIRTY YEARS now I have been studying my fellow men. I do not know very much about them. I should certainly hesitate to engage a servant on his face, and yet I suppose it is on the face that for the most part we judge the persons we meet. We draw our conclusions from the shape of the jaw, the look in the eyes, the contour of the mouth. I wonder if we are more often right than wrong. Why novels and plays are so often untrue to life is because their authors, perhaps of necessity, make their characters all of a piece. They cannot afford to make them self-contradictory, for then they become incomprehensible, and yet self-contradictory is what most of us are. We are a haphazard bundle of inconsistent qualities. In books on logic they will tell you that it is absurd to say that yellow is tubular or gratitude heavier than air; but in that mixture of incongruities that makes up the self yellow may very well be a horse and cart and gratitude the middle of next week. I shrug my shoulders when people tell me that their first impressions of a person are always right. I think they must have small insight or great vanity. For my own part I find that the longer I know people the more they puzzle me: my oldest friends are just those of whom I can say that I don't know the first thing about them.

These reflections have occurred to me because I read in this morning's paper that Edward Hyde Burton had died at Kobe. He was a merchant and he had been in business in Japan for many years. I knew him very little, but he interested me because once he gave me a great surprise. Unless I had heard the story from his own lips I should never have believed that he was capable of such an action. It was more startling because both in appearance and manner he suggested a very definite type. Here if ever was a man all of a piece. He was a tiny little fellow, not much more than five feet four in height, and very slender, with white hair, a red face much wrinkled, and blue eyes. I suppose he was about sixty when I knew him. He was always neatly and quietly dressed in accordance with his age and station.

Though his offices were in Kobe Burton often came down to Yokohama. I happened on one occasion to be spending a few days there, waiting for a ship, and I was introduced to him at the British Club. We played bridge together. He played a good game and a generous one. He did not talk very much, either then or later when we were having drinks, but what he said was sensible. He had a quiet, dry humour. He seemed to be popular at the club and afterwards, when he had gone, they described him as one of the best. It happened that we were both staying at the Grand Hotel and next day he asked me to dine with him. I met his wife, fat, elderly and smiling, and his two daughters. It was evidently a united and affectionate family. I think the chief thing that struck me about Burton was his kindliness. There was something very pleasing in his mild blue eyes. His voice was gentle; you could not imagine that he could possibly raise it in anger; his smile was benign. Here was a man who attracted you because you felt in him a real love for his fellows. He had charm. But there was nothing mawkish in him: he liked his game of cards and his cocktail, he could tell with point a good and spicy story, and in his youth he had been something of an athlete. He was a rich man and he had made every penny himself. I suppose one thing that made you like him was that he was so small and frail; he aroused your instincts of protection. You felt that he could not bear to hurt a fly.

One afternoon I was sitting in the lounge of the Grand Hotel. This was before the earthquake and they had leather armchairs there. From the windows you had a spacious view of the harbour with its crowded traffic. There were great liners on their way to Vancouver and San Francisco or to Europe by way of Shanghai, Hong-Kong and Singapore; there were tramps of all nations, battered and sea worn, junks with their high sterns and great coloured sails, and innumerable sampans. It was a busy, exhilarating scene, and yet, I know not why, restful to the spirit. Here was romance and it seemed that you had but to stretch out your hand to touch it.

Burton came into the lounge presently and caught sight of me. He seated himself in the chair next to mine.

"What do you say to a little drink?"

He clapped his hands for a boy and ordered two gin fizzes. As the boy brought them a man passed along the street outside and seeing me waved his hand.

"Do you know Turner?" said Burton as I nodded a greeting.

"I've met him at the club. I'm told he's a remittance man."

"Yes, I believe he is. We have a good many here."

"He plays bridge well."

"They generally do. There was a fellow here last year, oddly enough a namesake of mine, who was the best bridge player I ever met. I suppose you never came across him in London. Lenny Burton he called himself. I believe he'd belonged to some very good clubs."

"No, I don't believe I remember the name."

"He was quite a remarkable player. He seemed to have an instinct about the cards. It was uncanny. I used to play with him a lot. He was in Kobe for some time."

Burton sipped his gin fizz.

"It's rather a funny story," he said. "He wasn't a bad chap. I liked him. He was always well dressed and smart looking. He was handsome in a way, with curly hair and pink-and-white cheeks. Women thought a lot of him. There was no harm in him, you know, he was only wild. Of course he drank too much. Those sort of fellows always do. A bit of money used to come in for him once a quarter and he made a bit more by card playing. He won a good deal of mine, I know that."

Burton gave a kindly little chuckle. I knew from my own experience that he could lose money at bridge with a good grace. He stroked his shaven chin with his thin hand; the veins stood out on it and it was almost transparent.

"I suppose that is why he came to me when he went broke, that and the fact that he was a namesake of mine. He came to see me in my office one day and asked me for a job. I was rather surprised. He told me that there was no more money coming from home and he wanted to work. I asked him how old he was.

" 'Thirty-five,' he said.

" 'And what have you been doing hitherto?' I asked him.

" 'Well, nothing very much,' he said.

"I couldn't help laughing.

" 'I'm afraid I can't do anything for you just yet,' I said. 'Come back and see me in another thirty-five years, and I'll see what I can do.'

"He didn't move. He went rather pale. He hesitated for a moment and then he told me that he had had bad luck at cards for some time. He hadn't been willing to stick to bridge, he'd been playing poker, and he'd got trimmed. He hadn't a penny. He'd pawned everything he had. He couldn't pay his hotel bill and they wouldn't give him any more credit. He was down and out. If he couldn't get something to do he'd have to commit suicide.

"I looked at him for a bit. I could see now that he was all to pieces. He'd been drinking more than usual and he looked fifty. The girls wouldn't have thought so much of him if they'd seen him then.

" 'Well, isn't there anything you can do except play cards?' I asked him.

" 'I can swim,' he said.

" 'Swim!'

"I could hardly believe my ears; it seemed such an inane answer to give.

" 'I swam for my university.'

"I got some glimmering of what he was driving at. I've known too many men who were little tin gods at their university to be impressed by it.

" 'I was a pretty good swimmer myself when I was a young man,' I said.

"Suddenly I had an idea."

Pausing in his story, Burton turned to me.

"Do you know Kobe?" he asked.

"No," I said, "I passed through it once, but I only spent a night there."

"Then you don't know the Shioya Club. When I was a young man I swam from there round the beacon and landed at the creek of Tarumi. It's over three miles and it's rather difficult on account of the currents round the beacon. Well, I told my young namesake about it and I said to him that if he'd do it I'd give him a job.

"I could see he was rather taken aback.

" 'You say you're a swimmer,' I said.

" 'I'm not in very good condition,' he answered.

"I didn't say anything. I shrugged my shoulders. He looked at me for a moment and then he nodded.

" 'All right,' he said. 'When do you want me to do it?'

"I looked at my watch. It was just aften ten.

" 'The swim shouldn't take you much over an hour and a quarter. I'll drive round to the creek at half-past twelve and meet you. I'll take you back to the club to dress and then we'll have lunch together.'

" 'Done,' he said.

"We shook hands. I wished him good luck and he left me. I had a lot of work to do that morning and I only just managed to get to the creek at Tarumi at half-past twelve. But I needn't have hurried; he never turned up."

"Did he funk it at the last moment?" I asked.

"No, he didn't funk it. He started all right. But of course he'd ruined his constitution by drink and dissipation. The currents round the beacon were more than he could manage. We didn't get the body for about three days."

I didn't say anything for a moment or two. I was a trifle shocked. Then I asked Burton a question.

"When you made him that offer of a job, did you know he'd be drowned?"

He gave a little mild chuckle and he looked at me with those kind and candid blue eyes of his. He rubbed his chin with his hand.

"Well, I hadn't got a vacancy in my office at the moment."

# THE PORTRAIT OF A GENTLEMAN

I ARRIVED IN SEOUL towards evening, and after dinner, tired by the long railway journey from Peking, to stretch my cramped legs I went for a walk. I wandered at random along a narrow and busy street. The Koreans in their long white gowns and their little white top-hats were amusing to look at and the open shops displayed wares that arrested my foreign eyes. Presently I came to a second-hand bookseller's and catching sight of shelves filled with English books went in to have a look at them. I glanced at the titles and my heart sank. They were commentaries on the Old Testament, treatises on the Epistles of St Paul, sermons and lives of divines doubtless eminent, but whose names were unfamiliar to me; for I am an ignorant person. I supposed that this was the library of some missionary whom death had claimed in the midst of his labours and whose books then had been purchased by a Japanese bookseller. The Japanese are astute, but I could not imagine who in Seoul would be found to buy a work in three volumes on the Epistle to the Corinthians.

But as I was turning away, between volume two and volume three of this treatise I noticed a little book bound in paper. I do not know what induced me to take it out. It was called the Complete Poker Player and its cover was illustrated with a hand holding four aces. I looked at the title-page. The author was Mr John Blackbridge, actuary and counsellor-at-law, and the Preface was dated 1879. I wondered how this work happened to be among the books of a deceased missionary and I looked in one or two of them to see if I could find his name. Perhaps it was there only by accident. It may be that it was the entire library of a stranded gambler and had found its way to those shelves when his effects were sold to pay his hotel bill. But I preferred to think that it was indeed the property of the missionary and that when he was weary of reading divinity he rested his mind by the perusal of these lively pages. Perhaps somewhere in Korea, at night and alone in his mission house, he dealt innumerable poker hands in order to see for himself whether you could really only get a straight flush once in sixty-five thousand hands. But the owner of the shop was looking at me with disfavour so I turned to him and asked the price of the book. He gave it a contemptuous glance and told me I could have it for twenty sen. I put it in my pocket.

I do not remember that for so small a sum I have ever purchased better entertainment. For Mr John Blackbridge in these pages of his did a thing that no writer can do who deliberately tries to, but that, if done unconsciously, gives a book a rare and precious savour: he painted a complete portrait of himself. He stands before the reader so vividly that I was convinced that a woodcut of him figured as a frontispiece and I was surprised to discover, on looking at the book again the other day, that there was nothing of the kind. I see him very distinctly as a man of middle age, in a black frock-coat and a chimney-pot hat, wearing a black satin stock; he is clean-shaven and his jaw is square; his lips are thin and his eyes wary; his face is sallow and somewhat wrinkled. It is a countenance not without severity, but when he tells a story or makes one of his dry jokes his eyes light up and his smile is winning. He enjoyed his bottle of burgundy, but I cannot believe that he ever drank enough to confuse his excellent faculties. He was just rather than merciful at the card table and he was prepared to punish presumption with rigour. He had few illusions, for here are some of the things that life had taught him: "men hate those whom they have injured; men love those whom they have benefited; men naturally avoid their benefactors; men are universally actuated by self-interest; gratitude is a lively sense of expected benefits; promises are never forgotten by those to whom they are made, usually by those who make them."

It may be presumed that he was a Southerner, for while speaking of Jack Pots, which he describes as a frivolous attempt to make the game more interesting, he remarks that they are not popular in the South. "This last fact," he says, "contains much promise, because the South is the conservative portion of the country, and may be relied on as the last resort of good sense in social matters. The revolutionary Kossuth made no progress below Richmond; neither Spiritualism, nor Free Love, nor Communism, has ever been received with the least favour by the Southern mind; and it is for this reason that we greatly respect the Southern verdict upon the Jack Pot." It was in his day an innovation and he condemned it. "The time has arrived when all additions to the present standard combinations in Draw Poker must be worthless; the game being complete. The Jack Pot," he says, "was invented (in Toledo, Ohio) by reckless players to compensate losses incurred by playing against cautious players; and the principle is the same as if a party should play whist for stakes, and all be obliged every few minutes to stop, and purchase tickets in a lottery; or raffle for a turkey; or share a deal in Keno."

Poker is a game for gentlemen (he does not hesitate to make frequent use of this abused word; he lived in a day when to be a gentleman had its obligations but also its privileges) and a straight flush is to be respected, not because you make money on it ("I have never seen anyone make much money upon a straight flush," he says) but "because it prevents any hand from being *absolutely* the winning hand, and thus relieves gentlemen from the necessity of betting on a certainty. Without the use of straights, and hence without the use of a straight flush, four aces would be a certainty, and no gentleman could do more than *call* on them." This, I confess, catches me on the raw, for once in my life I had a straight flush and bet on it till I was called.

Mr John Blackbridge had personal dignity, rectitude, humour and common sense. "The amusements of mankind," he says, "have not as yet received proper recognition at the hands of the makers of the civil law, and of the unwritten social law," and he had no patience with the persons who condemn the most agreeable pastime that has been invented, namely gambling, because risk is attached to it. Every transaction in life is a risk, he truly observes, and involves the question of loss and gain. "To retire to rest at night is a practice that is fortified by countless precedents, and it is generally regarded as prudent and necessary. Yet it is surrounded by risks of every kind." He enumerates them and finally sums up his argument with these reasonable words: "If social circles welcome the banker and merchant who live by taking fair risks for the sake of profit, there is no apparent reason why they should not at least tolerate the man who at times employs himself in giving and taking fair risks for the sake of amusement." But here his good sense is obvious. "Twenty years of experience in the city of New York, both professionally" (you must not forget that he is an actuary and counsellor-at-law) "and as a student of social life, satisfy me that the average American gentleman in a large city has not over three thousand dollars a year to spend upon amusements. Will it be fair to devote more than one third of this fund to cards? I do not think that anyone will say that one third is not ample allowance for a single amusement. Given, therefore, a thousand dollars a year for the purpose of playing Draw Poker, what should be the limit of the stakes, in order that the average American gentleman may play the game with a contented mind, and with the certainty not only that he can pay his losses, but that his winnings will be paid to him?" Mr Blackbridge has no doubt that the answer is two dollars and a half. "The game of Poker should be intellectual and not emotional;

and it is impossible to exclude the emotions from it, if the stakes are so high that the question of loss and gain penetrates to the feelings." From this quotation it may be seen that Mr Blackbridge looked upon poker as only on the side a game of chance. He considered that it needed as much force of character, mental ability, power of decision and insight into motive to play poker as to govern a country or to lead an army, and I have an idea that on the whole he would have thought it a more sensible use of a man's faculties.

I am tempted to quote interminably, for Mr Blackbridge seldom writes a sentence that is other than characteristic, and his language is excellent: it is dignified as befits his subject and his condition (he does not forget that he is a gentleman), measured, clear and pointed. His phrase takes an ample sweep when he treats of mankind and its foibles, but he can be as direct and simple as you please. Could anything be better than this terse but adequate description of a card-sharper? "He was a very good-looking man of about forty years of age, having the appearance of one who had been leading a temperate and thoughtful life." But I will content myself with giving a few of his aphorisms and wise saws chosen almost at random from the wealth of his book.

"Let your chips talk for you. A silent player is so far forth, a mystery; and a mystery is always feared."

"In this game never do anything that you are not compelled to; while cheerfully responding to your obligations."

"At Draw Poker all statements not called for by the laws of the game, or supported by ocular demonstration, may be set down as fictitious; designed to enliven the path of truth throughout the game, as flowers in summer enliven the margins of the highway."

"Lost money is never recovered. After losing you may win, but the losing does not bring the winning."

"No gentleman will ever play any game of cards with the design of habitually winning and never losing."

"A gentleman is always willing to pay a fair price for recreation and amusement."

". . . that habit of mind which continually leads us to undervalue the mental force of other men, while we continually overvalue their good luck."

"The injury done to your capital by a loss is never compensated by the benefit done to your capital by a gain of the same amount."

"Players usually straddle when they are in bad

luck, upon the principle that bad play and bad luck united will win. A slight degree of intoxication aids to perfect this intellectual deduction."

"Euchre is a contemptible game."

"The lower cards as well as the lower classes are only useful in combination or in excess, and cannot be depended upon under any other circumstances."

"It is a hard matter to hold four Aces as steadily as a pair, but the table will bear their weight with as much equanimity as a pair of deuces."

Of good luck and bad luck: "To feel emotions over such incidents is unworthy of a man; and it is much more unworthy to express them. But no words need be wasted over practices which all men despise in others; and, in their reflecting moments, lament in themselves."

"Endorsing for your friends is a bad habit, but it is nothing to playing Poker on credit. . . . Debit and credit ought never to interfere with the fine intellectual calculations of this game."

There is a grand ring in his remarks on the player who has trained his intellect to bring logic to bear upon the principles and phenomena of the game. "He will thus feel a constant sense of security amid all possible fluctuations that occur, and he will also abstain from pressing an ignorant or an intellectually weak opponent, beyond what may be necessary either for the purpose of playing the game correctly, or of punishing presumption."

I leave Mr John Blackbridge with this last word and I can hear him saying it gently, but with a tolerant smile:

"For we must take human nature as it is."

# THE END OF THE FLIGHT

I SHOOK HANDS with the skipper and he wished me luck. Then I went down to the lower deck crowded with passengers, Malays, Chinese and Dyaks, and made my way to the ladder. Looking over the ship's side I saw that my luggage was already in the boat. It was a large, clumsy-looking craft, with a great square sail of bamboo matting, and it was crammed full of gesticulating natives. I scrambled in and a place was made for me. We were about three miles from the shore and a stiff breeze was blowing. As we drew near I saw that the coconut trees in a green abundance grew to the water's edge and among them I saw the brown roofs of the village. A Chinese who spoke English pointed out to me a white bungalow as the residence of the District Officer. Though he did not know it, it was with him that I was going to stay. I had a letter of introduction to him in my pocket.

I felt somewhat forlorn when I landed and my bags were set down beside me on the glistening beach. This was a remote spot to find myself in, this little town on the north coast of Borneo, and I felt a trifle shy at the thought of presenting myself to a total stranger with the announcement that I was going to sleep under his roof, eat his food and drink his whisky, till another boat came in to take mc to the port for which I was bound.

But I might have spared myself these misgivings, for the moment I reached the bungalow and sent in my letter he came out, a sturdy, ruddy, jovial man, of thirty-five perhaps, and greeted me with heartiness. While he held my hand he shouted to a boy to bring drinks and to another to look after my luggage. He cut short my apologies.

"Good God, man, you have no idea how glad I am to see you. Don't think I'm doing anything for you in putting you up. The boot's on the other leg. And stay as long as you damned well like. Stay a year."

I laughed. He put away his day's work, assuring me that he had nothing to do that could not wait till the morrow, and threw himself into a long chair. We talked and drank and talked. When the heat of the day wore off we went for a long tramp in the jungle and came back wet to the skin. A bath and a change were very grateful, and then we dined. I was tired out and though my host was plainly willing to go on talking straight through the night I was obliged to beg him to allow me to go to bed.

"All right, I'll just come along to your room and see everything's all right."

It was a large room with verandas on two sides of it, sparsely furnished, but with a huge bed protected by mosquito netting.

"The bed is rather hard. Do you mind?"

"Not a bit. I shall sleep without rocking to-night."

My host looked at the bed reflectively.

"It was a Dutchman who slept in it last. Do you want to hear a funny story?"

I wanted chiefly to go to bed, but he *was* my host, and being at times somewhat of a humorist myself I know that it is hard to have an amusing story to tell and find no listener.

"He came on the boat that brought you, on its last journey along the coast, he came into my office and asked where the dak bungalow was. I told him there wasn't one, but if he hadn't anywhere to go I didn't mind putting him up. He jumped at the invitation. I told him to have his kit sent along.

" 'This is all I've got,' he said.

"He held out a little shiny black grip. It seemed a bit scanty, but it was no business of mine, so I told him to go along to the bungalow and I'd come as soon as I was through with my work. While I was speaking the door of my office was opened and my clerk came in. The Dutchman had his back to the door and it may be that my clerk opened it a bit suddenly. Anyhow the Dutchman gave a shout, he jumped about two feet into the air and whipped out a revolver.

" 'What the hell are you doin'?' I said.

"When he saw it was the clerk he collapsed. He leaned against the desk, panting, and upon my word he was shaking as though he'd got fever.

" 'I beg your pardon,' he said. 'It's my nerves. My nerves are terrible.'

" 'It looks like it,' I said.

"I was rather short with him. To tell you the truth I wished I hadn't asked him to stop with me. He didn't look as though he'd been drinking a lot and I wondered if he was some fellow the police were after. If he were, I said to myself, he could hardly be such a fool as to walk right into the lion's den.

" 'You'd better go and lie down,' I said.

"He took himself off, and when I got back to my bungalow I found him sitting quite quietly, but bolt upright, on the veranda. He'd had a bath and shaved and put on clean things and he looked fairly presentable.

" 'Why are you sitting in the middle of the place like that?' I asked him. 'You'll be much more comfortable in one of the long chairs.'

" 'I prefer to sit up,' he said.

"Queer, I thought. But if a man in this heat would rather sit up than lie down it's his own lookout. He wasn't much to look at, tallish and heavily built, with a square head and close-cropped bristly hair. I should think he was about forty. The thing that chiefly struck me about him was his expression. There was a look in his eyes, blue eyes they were and rather small, that beat me altogether; and his face sagged as it were; it gave you the feeling he was going to cry. He had a way of looking quickly over his left shoulder as though he thought he heard something. By God, he was nervous. But we had a couple of drinks and he began to talk. He spoke English very well; except for a slight accent you'd never have known that he was a foreigner, and I'm bound to admit he was a good talker. He'd been everywhere and he'd read any amount. It was a treat to listen to him.

"We had three or four whiskies in the afternoon and a lot of gin pahits later on, so that when dinner came along we were by way of being rather hilarious and I'd come to the conclusion that he was a damned good fellow. Of course we had a lot of whisky at dinner and I happened to have a bottle of Benedictine, so we had some liqueurs afterwards. I can't help thinking we both got very tight.

"And at last he told me why he'd come. It was a rum story."

My host stopped and looked at me with his mouth slightly open as though, remembering it now, he was struck again with its rumness.

"He came from Sumatra, the Dutchman, and he'd done something to an Achinese and the Achinese had sworn to kill him. At first he made light of it, but the fellow tried two or three times and it began to be rather a nuisance, so he thought he'd better go away for a bit. He went over to Batavia and made up his mind to have a good time. But when he'd been there a week he saw the fellow slinking along a wall. By God, he'd followed him. It looked as though he meant business. The Dutchman began to think it was getting beyond a joke and he thought the best thing he could do was to skip off to Soerabaya. Well, he was strolling about there one day, you know how crowded the streets are, when he happened to turn round and saw the Achinese walking quite quietly just behind him. It gave him a turn. It would give anyone a turn.

"The Dutchman went straight back to his hotel, packed his things, and took the next boat to Singapore. Of course he put up at the Van Wyck, all the Dutch stay there, and one day when he was having a drink in the courtyard in front of the hotel, the Achinese walked in as bold as brass, looked at him for a minute, and walked out again. The Dutchman told me he was just paralyzed. The fellow could have stuck his kriss into him there and then and he wouldn't have been able to move a hand to defend himself. The Dutchman knew he was just biding his time, that damned native was going to kill him, he saw it in his eyes; and he went all to pieces."

"But why didn't he go to the police?" I asked.

"I don't know. I expect it wasn't a thing he wanted the police to be mixed up in."

"But what had he done to the man?"

"I don't know that either. He wouldn't tell me. But by the look he gave when I asked him, I expect it was something pretty rotten. I have an idea he knew he deserved whatever the Achinese could do."

My host lit a cigarette.

"Go on," I said.

"The skipper of the boat that runs between Singapore and Kuching lives at the Van Wyck between trips and the boat was starting at dawn. The Dutchman thought it a grand chance to give the fellow the slip; he left his luggage at the hotel and walked down to the ship with the skipper, as if he were just going to see him off, and stayed on her when she sailed. His nerves were all anyhow by then. He didn't care about anything but getting rid of the Achinese. He felt pretty safe at Kuching. He got a room at the rest-house and bought himself a couple of suits and some shirts in the Chinese shops. But he told me he couldn't sleep. He dreamt of that man and half a dozen times he awakened just as he thought a kriss was being drawn across his throat. By God, I felt quite sorry for him. He just shook as he talked to me and his voice was hoarse with terror. That was the meaning of the look I had noticed. You remember, I told you he had a funny look on his face and I couldn't tell what it meant. Well, it was fear.

"And one day when he was in the club at Kuching he looked out of the window and saw the Achinese sitting there. Their eyes met. The Dutchman just crumpled up and fainted. When he came to, his first idea was to get out. Well, you know, there's not a hell of a lot of traffic at Kuching and this boat that brought you was the only one that gave him a chance to get away quickly. He got on her. He was positive the man wasn't on board."

"But what made him come here?"

"Well, the old tramp stops at a dozen places on the coast and the Achinese couldn't possibly guess he'd chosen this one because he only made up his mind to get off when he saw there was only one boat to take the passengers ashore, and there weren't more than a dozen people in it.

" 'I'm safe here for a bit at all events,' he said, 'and if I can only be quiet for a while I shall get my nerve back.'

" 'Stay as long as you like,' I said. 'You're all right here, at all events till the boat comes along next month, and if you like we'll watch the people who come off.'

"He was all over me. I could see what a relief it was to him.

"It was pretty late and I suggested to him that we should turn in. I took him to his room to see that it was all right. He locked the door of the bathhouse and bolted the shutters, though I told him there was no risk, and when I left him I heard him lock the door I had just gone out of.

"Next morning when the boy brought me my tea I asked him if he'd called the Dutchman. He said he was just going to. I heard him knock and knock again. Funny, I thought. The boy hammered on the door, but there was no answer. I felt a little nervous, so I got up. I knocked too. We made enough noise to rouse the dead, but the Dutchman slept on. Then I broke down the door. The mosquito curtains were neatly tucked in round the bed. I pulled them apart. He was lying there on his back with his eyes wide open. He was as dead as mutton. A kriss lay across his throat, and say I'm a liar if you like, but I swear to God it's true, there wasn't a wound about him anywhere. The room was empty.

"Funny, wasn't it?"

"Well, that all depends on your idea of humour," I replied.

My host looked at me quickly.

"You don't mind sleeping in that bed, do you?"

"N-no. But I'd just as soon you'd told me the story tomorrow morning."

# THE JUDGEMENT SEAT

THEY AWAITED THEIR TURN patiently, but patience was no new thing to them; they had practised it, all three of them, with grim determination, for thirty years. Their lives had been a long preparation for this moment and they looked forward to the issue now, if not with self-confidence, for that on so awful an occasion would have been misplaced, at all events with hope and courage. They had taken the strait and narrow path when the flowery meads of sin stretched all too invitingly before them; with heads held high, though with breaking hearts, they had resisted temptation; and now, their arduous journey done, they expected their reward. There was no need for them to speak, since each knew the others' thoughts, and they felt that in all three of them the same emotion of relief filled their bodiless souls with thanksgiving. With what anguish now would they have been wrung if they had yielded to the passion which then had seemed so nearly irresistible and what a madness it would have been if for a few short years of bliss they had sacrificed that Life Everlasting which with so bright a light at long last shone before them! They felt like men who with the skin of their teeth have escaped a sudden and violent death and touch their feet and hands and, scarce able to believe that they are still alive, look about them in amazement. They had done nothing with which they could reproach themselves and when presently their angels came and told them that the moment was come, they would advance, as they had passed through the world that was now so far behind, happily conscious that they had done their duty. They stood a little on one side, for the press was great. A terrible war was in progress and for years the soldiers of all nations, men in the full flush of their gallant youth, had marched in an interminable procession to the Judgement Seat; women and children too, their lives brought to a wretched end by violence or, more unhappily, by grief, disease and starvation; and there was in the courts of heaven not a little confusion.

It was on account of this war, too, that these three wan, shivering ghosts stood in expectation of their doom. For John and Mary had been passengers on a ship which was sunk by the torpedo of a submarine; and Ruth, broken in health by the arduous work to which she had so nobly devoted herself, hearing of the death of the man whom she had loved with all her heart, sank beneath the blow and died. John, indeed, might have saved himself if he had not tried to save his wife; he hated her; he had hated her to the depths of his soul for thirty years; but he had always done his duty by her and now, in the moment of dreadful peril, it never occurred to him that he could do otherwise.

At last their angels took them by the hand and led them to the Presence. For a little while the Eternal took not the slightest notice of them. If the truth must be told he was in a bad humour. A moment before there had come up for judgement a philosopher, deceased full of years and honours, who had told the Eternal to his face that he did not believe in him. It was not this that would have disturbed the serenity of the King of Kings, this could only have made him smile; but the philosopher, taking perhaps an unfair advantage of the regrettable happenings just then upon Earth, had asked him how, considering them dispassionately, it was possible to reconcile his All-Power with his All-Goodness.

"No one can deny the fact of Evil," said the philosopher, sententiously. "Now, if God cannot prevent Evil he is not all-powerful, and if he can prevent it and will not, he is not all-good."

This argument was of course not new to the Omniscient, but he had always refused to consider the matter; for the fact is, though he knew everything, he did not know the answer to this. Even God cannot make two and two five. But the philosopher, pressing his advantage, and, as philosophers often will, drawing from a reasonable premise an unjustifiable inference, the philosopher had finished with a statement that in the circumstances was surely preposterous.

"I will not believe," he said, "in a God who is not All-Powerful and All-Good."

It was not then perhaps without relief that the Eternal turned his attention to the three shades who stood humbly and yet hopefully before him. The quick, with so short a time to live, when they talk of themselves, talk too much; but the dead, with eternity before them, are so verbose that only angels could listen to them with civility. But this in brief is the story that these three recounted. John and Mary had been happily married for five years and till John met Ruth they loved each other, as married couples for the most part do, with sincere affection and mutual respect. Ruth was eighteen, ten years younger than he was, a charming, graceful animal, with a sudden and all-conquering loveliness; she was as healthy in mind as she was in body, and, eager for the natural happiness of life, was capable of achieving that greatness which is beauty of soul. John fell in love with her and she with him. But it was no ordinary passion that seized them; it was something so overwhelming that they felt as if the whole long history of the world signified only because it had led to the time and place that had brought them together. They loved as Daphnis and Chloe or as Paolo and Francesca. But after that first moment of ecstasy when each discovered the other's love they were seized with dismay. They were decent people and they respected themselves, the beliefs in which they had been bred, and the society in which they lived. How could he betray an innocent girl and what had she to do with a married man? Then they grew conscious that Mary was aware of their love. The confident affection with which she had regarded her husband was shaken; and there arose in her feelings of which she would never have thought herself capable, jealousy and the fear that he would desert her, anger because her possession of his heart was threatened and a strange hunger of the soul which was more painful than love. She felt that she would die if he left her; and yet she knew that if he loved it was because love had come to him, not because he had sought it. She did not blame him. She prayed for strength; she wept silent, bitter tears. John and Ruth saw her pine away before their eyes. The struggle was long and bitter. Sometimes their hearts failed them and they felt that they could not resist the passion that burned the marrow of their bones. They resisted. They wrestled with evil as Jacob wrestled with the angel of God and at last they conquered. With breaking hearts, but proud in their innocence, they parted. They offered up to God, as it were a sacrifice, their hopes of happiness, the joy of life and the beauty of the world.

Ruth had loved too passionately ever to love again and with a stony heart she turned to God and to good works. She was indefatigable. She tended the sick and assisted the poor. She founded orphanages and managed charitable institutions. And little by little her beauty which she cared for no longer left her and her face grew as hard as her heart. Her religion was fierce and narrow; her very kindness was cruel because it was founded not on love but on reason; she became domineering, intolerant and vindictive. And John resigned, but sullen and angry, dragged himself along the weary years waiting for the release of death. Life lost its meaning to him; he had made his effort and in conquering was conquered; the only emotion that remained with him was the unceasing, secret hatred with which he looked upon his wife. He used her with kindness and consideration; he did everything that could be expected of a man who was a Christian and a gentleman. He did his duty. Mary, a good, faithful and (it must be confessed) exceptional wife, never thought to reproach her husband for the madness that had seized him; but all the same she could not forgive him for the sacrifice he had made for her sake. She grew acid and querulous. Though she hated herself for it, she could not refrain from saying the things that she knew would wound him. She would willingly have sacrificed her life for him, but she could not bear that he should enjoy a moment's happiness when she was so wretched that a hundred times she had wished she was dead. Well, now she was and so were they; grey and drab had life been, but that was past; they had not sinned and now their reward was at hand.

They finished and there was silence. There was silence in all the courts of heaven. Go to hell were the words that came to the Eternal's lips, but he did not utter them, for they had a colloquial association that he rightly thought unfitting to the solemnity of the occasion. Nor indeed would such a decree have met the merits of the case. But his brow darkened. He asked himself if it was for this that he had made the rising sun shine on the boundless sea and the snow glitter on the mountain tops; was it for this that the brooks sang blithely as they hastened down the hillsides and the golden corn waved in the evening breeze?

"I sometimes think," said the Eternal, "that the stars never shine more brightly than when reflected in the muddy waters of a wayside ditch."

But the three shades stood before him and now that they had unfolded their unhappy story they could not but feel a certain satisfaction. It had been a bitter struggle, but they had done their duty. The Eternal blew lightly, he blew as a man might blow out a lighted match, and, behold! where the three poor souls had stood—was nothing. The Eternal annihilated them.

"I have often wondered why men think I attach so much importance to sexual irregularity," he said. "If they read my works more attentively they would see that I have always been sympathetic to that particular form of human frailty."

Then he turned to the philosopher who was still waiting for a reply to his remarks.

"You cannot but allow," said the Eternal, "that on this occasion I have very happily combined my All-Power with my All-Goodness."

# THE ANT AND THE GRASSHOPPER

When I was a very small boy I was made to learn by heart certain of the fables of La Fontaine, and the moral of each was carefully explained to me. Among those I learnt was The Ant and the Grasshopper which is devised to bring home to the young the useful lesson that in an imperfect world industry is rewarded and giddiness punished. In this admirable fable (I apologize for telling something which everyone is politely, but inexactly, supposed to know) the ant spends a laborious summer gathering its winter store, while the grasshopper sits on a blade of grass singing to the sun. Winter comes and the ant is comfortably provided for, but the grasshopper has an empty larder: he goes to the ant and begs for a little food. Then the ant gives him her classic answer:

"What were you doing in the summer time?"

"Saving your presence, I sang, I sang all day, all night."

"You sang. Why, then go and dance."

I do not ascribe it to perversity on my part, but rather to the inconsequence of childhood, which is deficient in moral sense, that I could never quite reconcile myself to the lesson. My sympathies were with the grasshopper and for some time I never saw an ant without putting my foot on it. In this summary (and as I have discovered since, entirely human) fashion I sought to express my disapproval of prudence and common sense.

I could not help thinking of this fable when the other day I saw George Ramsay lunching by himself in a restaurant. I never saw anyone wear an expression of such deep gloom. He was staring into space. He looked as though the burden of the whole world sat on his shoulders. I was sorry for him: I suspected at once that his unfortunate brother had been causing trouble again. I went up to him and held out my hand.

"How are you?" I asked.

"I'm not in hilarious spirits."

"Is it Tom again?"

He sighed.

"Yes, it's Tom again."

"Why don't you chuck him? You've done everything in the world for him. You must know by now that he's quite hopeless."

I suppose every family has a black sheep. Tom had been a sore trial to his for twenty years. He had begun life decently enough: he went into business, married and had two children. The Ramsays were perfectly respectable people and there was every reason to suppose that Tom Ramsay would have a useful and honourable career. But one day, without warning, he announced that he didn't like work and that he wasn't suited for marriage. He wanted to enjoy himself. He would listen to no expostulations. He left his wife and his office. He had a little money and he spent two happy years in the various capitals of Europe. Rumours of his doings reached his relations from time to time and they were profoundly shocked. He certainly had a very good time. They shook their heads and asked what would happen when his money was spent. They soon found out: he borrowed. He was charming and unscrupulous. I have never met anyone to whom it was more difficult to refuse a loan. He made a steady income from his friends and he made friends easily. But he always said that the money you spent on necessities was boring; the money that was amusing to spend was the money you spent in luxuries. For this he depended on his brother George. He did not waste his charm on him. George was a serious man and insensible to such enticements. George was respectable. Once or twice he fell to Tom's promises of amendment and gave him considerable sums in order that he might make a fresh start. On these Tom bought a motorcar and some very nice jewelry. But when circumstances forced George to realize that his brother would never settle down and he washed his hands of him, Tom, without a qualm, began to blackmail him. It was not very nice for a respectable lawyer to find his brother shaking cocktails behind the bar of his favourite restaurant or to see him waiting on the box seat of a taxi outside his club. Tom said that to serve in a bar or to drive a taxi was a perfectly decent occupation, but if George could oblige him with a couple of hundred pounds he didn't mind for the honour of the family giving it up. George paid.

Once Tom nearly went to prison. George was terribly upset. He went into the whole discreditable affair. Really Tom had gone too far. He had been wild, thoughtless and selfish, but he had never before done anything dishonest, by which George meant illegal; and if he were prosecuted he would assuredly be convicted. But you cannot allow your only brother to go to gaol. The man Tom had cheated, a man called Cronshaw, was vindictive. He was determined to take the matter into court; he said Tom was a scoundrel and should be punished. It cost George an infinite deal of trouble and five hundred pounds to settle the affair. I have never seen him in such a rage as when he heard that Tom and Cronshaw had gone off together to Monte Carlo the moment they cashed the cheque. They spent a happy month there.

For twenty years Tom raced and gambled, philandered with the prettiest girls, danced, ate in the most expensive restaurants, and dressed beautifully. He always looked as if he had just stepped out of a bandbox. Though he was forty-six you would never have taken him for more than thirty-five. He was a most amusing companion and though you knew he was perfectly worthless you could not but enjoy his society. He had high spirits, an unfailing gaiety and incredible charm. I never grudged the contributions he regularly levied on me for the necessities of his existence. I never lent him fifty pounds without feeling that I was in his debt. Tom Ramsay knew everyone and everyone knew Tom Ramsay. You could not approve of him, but you could not help liking him.

Poor George, only a year older than his scapegrace brother, looked sixty. He had never taken more than a fortnight's holiday in the year for a quarter of a century. He was in his office every morning at nine-thirty and never left it till six. He was honest, industrious and worthy. He had a good wife, to whom he had never been unfaithful even in thought, and four daughters to whom he was the best of fathers. He made a point of saving a third of his income and his plan was to retire at fifty-five to a little house in the country where he proposed to cultivate his garden and play golf. His life was blameless. He was glad that he was growing old because Tom was growing old too. He rubbed his hands and said:

"It was all very well when Tom was young and good-looking, but he's only a year younger than I am. In four years he'll be fifty. He won't find life so easy then. I shall have thirty thousand pounds by the time I'm fifty. For twenty-five years I've said that Tom would end in the gutter. And we shall see how he likes that. We shall see if it really pays best to work or be idle."

Poor George! I sympathized with him. I wondered now as I sat down beside him what infamous thing Tom had done. George was evidently very much upset.

"Do you know what's happened now?" he asked me.

I was prepared for the worst. I wondered if Tom had got into the hands of the police at last. George could hardly bring himself to speak.

"You're not going to deny that all my life I've been hard-working, decent, respectable and straightforward. After a life of industry and thrift I can look forward to retiring on a small income in gilt-edged securities. I've always done my duty in that state of life in which it has pleased Providence to place me."

"True."

"And you can't deny that Tom has been an idle, worthless, dissolute and dishonourable rogue. If there were any justice he'd be in the workhouse."

"True."

George grew red in the face.

"A few weeks ago he became engaged to a woman old enough to be his mother. And now she's died and left him everything she had. Half a million pounds, a yacht, a house in London and a house in the country."

George Ramsay beat his clenched fist on the table.

"It's not fair, I tell you, it's not fair. Damn it, it's not fair."

I could not help it. I burst into a shout of laughter as I looked at George's wrathful face, I rolled in my chair, I very nearly fell on the floor. George never forgave me. But Tom often asks me to excellent dinners in his charming house in Mayfair and if he occasionally borrows a trifle from me that is merely force of habit. It is never more than a sovereign.

# FRENCH JOE

It was Captain Bartlett who told me of him. I do not think that many people have been to Thursday Island. It is in the Torres Straits and is so called because it was discovered on a Thursday by Captain Cook. I went there since they told me in Sydney that it was the last place God ever made. They said there was nothing to see and warned me that I should probably get my throat cut. I had come up from Sydney in a Japanese tramp and they put me ashore in a small boat. It was the middle of the night and there was not a soul on the jetty. One of the sailors who landed my kit told me that if I turned to the left I should presently come to a two-story building and this was the hotel. The boat pushed off and I was left alone. I do not much like being separated from my luggage, but I like still less to pass the night on a jetty and sleep on hard stones; so I shouldered a bag and set out. It was pitch dark. I seemed to walk much more than a few hundred yards which they had spoken of and was afraid I had missed my way, but at last saw dimly a building which seemed to be important enough to suggest that it might be the hotel. No light showed, but my eyes by now were pretty well accustomed to the darkness and I found a door. I struck a match, but could see no bell. I knocked; there was no reply; I knocked again, with my stick, as loudly as I could, then a window above me was opened and a woman's voice asked me what I wanted.

"I've just got off the Shika Maru," I said. "Can I have a room?"

"I'll come down."

I waited a little longer and the door was opened by a woman in a red flannel dressing-gown. Her hair was hanging over her shoulders in long black wisps. In her hand she held a paraffin lamp. She greeted me warmly, a little stoutish woman with keen eyes and a nose suspiciously red, and bade me come in. She took me upstairs and showed me a room.

"Now you sit down," she said, "and I'll make up the bed before you can say Jack Robinson. What will you 'ave? A drop of whisky would do you good, I should think. You won't want to be washing at this time of night, I'll bring you a towel in the morning."

And while she made the bed she asked me who I was and what I had come to Thursday Island for. She could see I wasn't a seafaring man—all the pilots came to this hotel and had done for twenty years—and she didn't know what business could have brought me. I wasn't that fellow as was coming to inspect the customs, was I? She'd 'eard they were sending someone from Sydney. I asked her if there were any pilots staying there then. Yes, there was one, Captain Bartlett, did I know him? A queer fish he was and no mistake. Hadn't got a hair on his head, but the way he could put his liquor away, well, it was a caution. There, the bed was ready and she expected I'd sleep like a top and one thing she could say was, the sheets were clean. She lit the end of a candle and bade me good-night.

Captain Bartlett certainly was a queer fish, but he is of no moment to my present purpose; I made his acquaintance at dinner next day—before I left Thursday Island I had eaten turtle soup so often that I have ceased to look upon it as a luxury—and it was because in the course of conversation I mentioned that I spoke French that he asked me to go and see French Joe.

"It'll be a treat to the old fellow to talk his own lingo for a bit. He's ninety-three, you know."

For the last two years, not because he was ill but because he was old and destitute, he had lived in the hospital and it was here that I visited him. He was lying in bed, in flannel pyjamas much too large for him, a little shrivelled old man with vivacious eyes, a short white beard and bushy black eyebrows. He was glad to speak French with me, which he spoke with the marked accent of his native isle, for he was a Corsican, but he had dwelt so many years among English-speaking people that he no longer spoke his mother-tongue with accuracy. He used English words as though they were French, making verbs of them with French terminations. He talked very quickly, with broad gestures, and his voice for the most part was clear and strong; but now and then it seemed suddenly to fade away so that it sounded as though he spoke from the grave. The hushed and hollow sound gave me an eery feeling. Indeed I could not look upon him still as of this world. His real name was Joseph de Paoli. He was a nobleman and a gentleman. He was of the same family as the general we have all read of in Boswell's Johnson, but he showed no interest in his famous ancestor.

"We have had so many generals in our family," he said. "You know, of course, that Napoleon Bonaparte was a connection of mine. No, I have never read Boswell. I have not read books. I have lived."

He had entered the French army in 1851. Seventy-five years ago. It is terrifying. As a lieutenant of artillery ("like my cousin Bonaparte," he said) he had fought the Russians in the Crimea, and as a captain, the Prussians in 1870. He showed me a scar on his bald pate from an Uhlan's lance and then with a dramatic gesture told how he had thrust his sword in the Uhlan's body with such violence that he could not withdraw it. The Uhlan fell dead and the sword remained in the body. But the Empire perished and he joined the Communists. For six weeks he fought against the government troops under Monsieur Thiers. To me Thiers is but a shadowy figure, and it was startling and even a trifle comic to hear French Joe speak with passionate hatred of a man who has been dead for half a century. His voice rose into a shrill scream as he repeated the insults, oriental in their imagery, which in the council he had flung at the head of this mediocre statesman. French Joe was tried and sentenced to five years in New Caledonia.

"They should have shot me," he said, "but, dirty cowards, they dared not."

Then came the long journey in a sailing vessel, and the antipodes, and his wrath flamed out again when he spoke of the indignity thrust upon him, a political prisoner, when they herded him with vulgar criminals. The ship put in at Melbourne and one of the officers, a fellow Corsican, enabled him to slip over the side. He swam ashore and, taking his friend's advice, went straight to the police station. No one there could understand a word he said, but an interpreter was sent for, his dripping papers were examined and he was told that so long as he did not set foot on a French ship he was safe.

"Freedom," he cried to me. "Freedom."

Then came a long series of adventures. He cooked, taught French, swept streets, worked in the gold mines, tramped, starved, and at last found his way to New Guinea. Here he underwent the most astonishing of his experiences, for drifting into the savage interior, and they are cannibals there still, after a hundred desperate adventures and hair-breadth escapes he made himself king of some wild tribe.

"Look at me, my friend," he said, "I who lie here on a hospital bed, the object of charity, have been monarch of all I surveyed. Yes, it is something to say that I have been a king."

But eventually he came into collision with the British and his sovereignty passed from him. He fled the country and started life once more. It is clear that he was a fellow of resource, for eventually he came to own a fleet of pearling luggers on Thursday Island. It looked as though at last he had reached a haven of peace and, an elderly man now, he looked forward to a prosperous and even respectable old age. A hurricane destroyed his boats and ruin fell upon him. He never recovered. He was too old to make a fresh start and since then had earned as best he could a precarious livelihood till at last, beaten, he had accepted the hospital's kindly shelter.

"But why did you not go back to France or Corsica? An amnesty was granted to the Communists a quarter of a century ago."

"What are France and Corsica to me after fifty years? A cousin of mine seized my land. We Corsicans never forget and never forgive. If I had gone back I should have had to kill him. He had his children."

"Funny old French Joe," smiled the hospital nurse who stood at the end of the bed.

"At all events you have had a fine life," I said.

"Never. Never. I have had a frightful life. Misfortune has followed me wherever I have turned my steps, and look at me now: I am rotten, fit for nothing but the grave. I thank God that I had no children to inherit the curse that is upon me."

"Why, Joe, I thought you didn't believe in God," said the nurse.

"It is true. I am a sceptic. I have never seen a sign that there is in the scheme of things an intelligent purpose. If the universe is the contrivance of some being, that being can only be a criminal imbecile." He shrugged his shoulders. "Anyhow I have not got much longer in this filthy world and then I shall go and see for myself what is the real truth of the whole business."

The nurse told me it was time to leave the old man and I took his hand to bid him farewell. I asked him if there was anything I could do for him.

"I want nothing," he said. "I only want to die." His black shining eyes twinkled. "But meanwhile I should be grateful for a packet of cigarettes."

# THE MAN WITH THE SCAR

IT WAS ON ACCOUNT of the scar that I first noticed him, for it ran, broad and red, in a great crescent from his temple to his chin. It must have been due to a formidable wound and I wondered whether this had been caused by a sabre or by a fragment of shell. It was unexpected on that round, fat and good-humoured face. He had small and undistinguished features, and his expression was artless. His face went oddly with his corpulent body. He was a powerful man of more than common height. I never saw him in anything but a very shabby grey suit, a khaki shirt and a battered sombrero. He was far from clean. He used to come into the Palace Hotel at Guatemala City every day at cocktail time and strolling leisurely round the bar offer lottery tickets for sale. If this was the way he made his living it must have been a poor one, for I never saw anyone buy, but now and then I saw him offered a drink. He never refused it. He threaded his way among the tables with a sort of rolling walk as though he were accustomed to traverse long distances on foot, paused at each table, with a little smile mentioned the numbers he had for sale and then, when no notice was taken of him, with the same smile passed on. I think he was for the most part a trifle the worse for liquor.

I was standing at the bar one evening, my foot on the rail, with an acquaintance—they make a very good dry martini at the Palace Hotel in Guatemala City—when the man with the scar came up. I shook my head as for the twentieth time since my arrival he held out for my inspection his lottery tickets. But my companion nodded affably.

"Qué tal, general? How is life?"

"Not so bad. Business is none too good, but it might be worse."

"What will you have, general?"

"A brandy."

He tossed it down and put the glass back on the bar. He nodded to my acquaintance.

"Gracias. Hasta luego."

Then he turned away and offered his tickets to the men who were standing next to us.

"Who is your friend?" I asked. "That's a terrific scar on his face."

"It doesn't add to his beauty, does it? He's an exile from Nicaragua. He's a ruffian of course and a bandit, but not a bad fellow. I give him a few pesos now and then. He was a revolutionary general and if his ammunition hadn't given out he'd have upset the government and be minister of war now instead of selling lottery tickets in Guatemala. They captured him, along with his staff, such as it was, and tried him by court-martial. Such things are rather summary in these countries, you know, and he was sentenced to be shot at dawn. I guess he knew what was coming to him when he was caught. He spent the night in gaol and he and the others, there were five of them altogether, passed the time playing poker. They used matches for chips. He told me he'd never had such a run of bad luck in his life; they were playing with a short pack, Jacks to open, but he never held a card; he never improved more than half a dozen times in the whole sitting and no sooner did he buy a new stack than he lost it. When day broke and the soldiers came into the cell to fetch them for execution he had lost more matches than a reasonable man could use in a lifetime.

"They were led into the patio of the gaol and placed against a wall, the five of them side by side, with the firing party facing them. There was a pause and our friend asked the officer in charge of them what the devil they were keeping him waiting for. The officer said that the general commanding the government troops wished to attend the execution and they awaited his arrival.

" 'Then I have time to smoke another cigarette,' said our friend. 'He was always unpunctual.'

"But he had barely lit it when the general—it was San Ignacio, by the way: I don't know whether you ever met him—followed by his A.D.C. came into the patio. The usual formalities were performed and San Ignacio asked the condemned men whether there was anything they wished before the execution took place. Four of the five shook their heads, but our friend spoke.

" 'Yes, I should like to say good-bye to my wife.'

" 'Bueno,' said the general, 'I have no objection to that. Where is she?'

" 'She is waiting at the prison door.'

" 'Then it will not cause a delay of more than five minutes.'

" 'Hardly that, Señor General.'

" 'Have him placed on one side.'

"Two soldiers advanced and between them the condemned rebel walked to the spot indicated. The officer in command of the firing squad on a nod from the general gave an order, there was a ragged report, and the four men fell. They fell strangely, not together, but one after the other, with movements that were almost grotesque, as though they were puppets in a toy theatre. The officer went up to them and into one who was still alive emptied two chambers of his revolver. Our friend finished his cigarette and threw away the stub.

"There was a little stir at the gateway. A woman came into the patio, with quick steps, and then, her hand on her heart, stopped suddenly. She gave a cry and with outstretched arms ran forward.

" 'Caramba,' said the general.

"She was in black, with a veil over her hair, and her face was dead white. She was hardly more than a girl, a slim creature, with little regular features and enormous eyes. But they were distraught with anguish. Her loveliness was such that as she ran, her mouth slightly open and the agony of her face beautiful, a gasp of surprise was wrung from those indifferent soldiers who looked at her.

"The rebel advanced a step or two to meet her. She flung herself into his arms and with a hoarse cry of passion: alma de mi corazón, soul of my heart, he pressed his lips to hers. And at the same moment he drew a knife from his ragged shirt—I haven't a notion how he had managed to retain possession of it—and stabbed her in the neck. The blood spurted from the cut vein and dyed his shirt. Then he flung his arms round her and once more pressed his lips to hers.

"It happened so quickly that many didn't know what had occurred, but from the others burst a cry of horror; they sprang forward and seized him. They loosened his grasp and the girl would have fallen if the A.D.C. hadn't caught her. She was unconscious. They laid her on the ground and with dismay on their faces stood round watching her. The rebel knew where he was striking and it was impossible to staunch the blood. In a moment the A.D.C. who had been kneeling by her side rose.

" 'She's dead,' he whispered.

"The rebel crossed himself.

" 'Why did you do it?' asked the general.

" 'I loved her.'

"A sort of sigh passed through those men crowded together and they looked with strange faces at the murderer. The general stared at him for a while in silence.

" 'It was a noble gesture,' he said at last. 'I cannot execute this man. Take my car and have him led to the frontier. Señor, I offer you the homage which is due from one brave man to another.'

"A murmur of approbation broke from those who listened. The A.D.C. tapped the rebel on the shoulder, and between the two soldiers without a word he marched to the waiting car."

My friend stopped and for a little I was silent. I must explain that he was a Guatemaltecan and spoke to me in Spanish. I have translated what he told me as well as I could, but I have made no attempt to tone down his rather high-flown language. To tell the truth I think it suits the story.

"But how then did he get the scar?" I asked at length.

"Oh, that was due to a bottle that burst when he was opening it. A bottle of ginger ale."

"I never liked it," said I.

# THE POET

I AM NOT MUCH INTERESTED in the celebrated and I have never had patience with the passion that afflicts so many to shake hands with the great ones of the earth. When it is proposed to me to meet some person distinguished above his fellows by his rank or his attainments, I seek for a civil excuse that may enable me to avoid the honour; and when my friend Diego Torre suggested giving me an introduction to Santa Ana I declined. But for once the excuse I made was sincere; Santa Ana was not only a great poet but also a romantic figure and it would have amused me to see in his decrepitude a man whose adventures (in Spain at least) were legendary; but I knew that he was old and ill and I could not believe that it would be anything but a nuisance to him to meet a stranger and a foreigner. Calisto de Santa Ana was the last descendant of the Grand School; in a world unsympathetic to Byronism he had led a Byronic existence and he had narrated his hazardous life in a series of poems that had brought him a fame unknown to his contemporaries. I am no judge of their value, for I read them first when I was three and twenty and then was enraptured by them; they had a passion, a heroic arrogance and a multi-coloured vitality that swept me off my feet, and to this day, so intermingled are those ringing lines and haunting cadences with the charming memories of my youth, I cannot read them without a beating heart. I am inclined to think that Calisto de Santa Ana deserves the reputation he enjoys among the Spanish-speaking peoples. In those days his verses were on the lips of all young men and my friends would talk to me endlessly of his wild ways, his vehement speeches (for he was a politician as well as a poet), his incisive wit and his amours. He was a rebel and sometimes an outlaw, daring and adventurous; but above all he was a lover. We knew all about his passion for this great actress or that divine singer—had we not read till we knew them by heart the burning sonnets in which he described his love, his anguish and his wrath?—and we were aware that an infanta of Spain, the proudest descendant of the Bourbons, having yielded to his entreaties, had taken the veil when he ceased to love her. When the Philips, her royal ancestors, tired of a mistress she entered a convent, for it was unfitting that one whom the King had loved should be loved by another, and was not Calisto de Santa Ana greater than any earthly king? We applauded the lady's romantic gesture; it was creditable to her and flattering to our poet.

But all this took place many years ago and for a quarter of a century Don Calisto, disdainfully withdrawing from a world that had nothing more to offer, had lived in seclusion in his native town of Ecija. It was when I announced my intention of going there (I had been spending a week or two in Seville) not because of him, but because it is a charming little Andalusian town with associations that endear it to me, that Diego Torre offered me this introduction. It appeared that Don Calisto allowed the younger men of letters occasionally to visit him and now and then would talk to them with the fire that had electrified his hearers in the great days of his prime.

"What does he look like now?" I asked.

"Magnificent."

"Have you a photograph of him?"

"I wish I had. He has refused to face the camera since he was thirty-five. He says he does not wish posterity to know him other than young."

I confess that I found this suggestion of vanity not a little touching. I knew that in early manhood he was of extraordinary beauty, and that moving sonnet of his written when he grew conscious that youth had for ever left him shows with what a bitter and sardonic pang he must have watched the passing of those looks that had been so fantastically admired.

But I refused my friend's offer; I was quite satisfied to read once more the poems I had known so well and for the rest I preferred to wander about the silent and sunswept streets of Ecija in freedom. It was with some consternation therefore that on the evening of my arrival I received a note from the great man himself. Diego Torre had written to him of my visit, he said, and it would give him great pleasure if I would call on him at eleven next morning. In the circumstances there was nothing for me to do but to present myself at his house at the appointed hour.

My hotel was in the Plaza and on that spring morning it was animated, but as soon as I left it I might have walked in a deserted city. The streets, the tortuous white streets, were empty but for a woman in black now and then who returned with measured steps from her devotions. Ecija is a town of churches and you can seldom go far without seeing a crumbling façade or a tower in which storks have built their nests. Once I paused to watch a string of little donkeys pass by. Their red caparisons were faded and they carried I know not what in their panniers. But Ecija has been a place of consequence in its day and many of these white houses have gateways of stone surmounted by imposing coats of arms, for to this remote spot flowed the riches of the New World and adventurers who had gathered wealth in the Americas spent here their declining years. It was in one of these houses that Don Calisto lived and as I stood at the reja after pulling the bell, I was pleased to think that he lived in such a fitting style. There was a dilapidated grandeur about the massive gateway that suited my impression of the flamboyant poet. Though I heard the bell peal through the house no one answered it and I rang a second and then a third time: at last an old woman with a heavy moustache came to the gate.

"What do you want?" she asked.

She had fine black eyes, but a sullen look, and I supposed that it was she who took care of the old man. I gave her my card.

"I have an appointment with your master."

She opened the iron gateway and bade me enter. Asking me to wait she left me and went upstairs. The patio was pleasantly cool after the street. Its proportions were noble and you surmised that it had been built by some follower of the conquistadores; but the paint was tarnished, the tiles on the floor broken, and here and there great flakes of plaster had fallen away. There was about everything an air of poverty but not of squalor. I knew that Don Calisto was poor. Money had come to him easily at times but he had never attached any importance to it and had spent it profusely. It was plain that he lived now in a penury that he disdained to notice. In the middle of the patio was a table with a rocking chair on each side of it, and on the table newspapers a fortnight old. I wondered what dreams occupied his fancy as he sat there on the warm summer nights, smoking cigarettes. On the walls under the colonnade were Spanish pictures, dark and bad, and here and there stood an ancient dusty bargueño and on it a mended lustre plate. By the side of a door hung a pair of old pistols, and I had a pleasant fancy that they were the weapons he had used when in the most celebrated of his many duels, for the sake of Pepa Montañez the dancer (now, I suppose, a toothless and raddled hag) he had killed the Duke of Dos Hermanos.

The scene, with its associations which I vaguely divined, so aptly fitted the romantic poet that I was overcome by the spirit of the place. Its noble indigence surrounded him with a glory as great as the magnificence of his youth; in him too there was the spirit of the old conquistadores and it was becoming that he should finish his famous life in that ruined and magnificent house. Thus surely should a poet live and die. I had arrived cool enough and even somewhat bored at the prospect of my meeting, but now I began to grow a trifle nervous. I lit a cigarette. I had come at the time appointed and wondered what detained the old man. The silence was strangely disturbing. Ghosts of the past thronged the silent patio and an age dead and gone gained a sort of shadowy life for me. The men of that day had a passion and a wildness of spirit that are gone out of the world for ever. We are no longer capable of their reckless deeds or their theatrical heroics.

I heard a sound and my heart beat quickly. I was excited now and when at last I saw him coming slowly down the stairs I caught my breath. He held my card in his hand. He was a tall old man and exceedingly thin, with a skin the colour of old ivory; his hair was abundant and white, but his bushy eyebrows were dark still; they made his great eyes flash with a more sombre fire. It was wonderful that at his age those black eyes should still preserve their brilliance. His nose was aquiline, his mouth close set. His unsmiling eyes rested on me as he approached and there was in them a look of cool appraisal. He was dressed in black and in one hand held a broad-brimmed hat. There was in his bearing assurance and dignity. He was as I should have wished him to be and as I watched him I understood how he had swayed men's minds and touched their hearts. He was every inch a poet.

He reached the patio and came slowly towards me. He had really the eyes of an eagle. It seemed to me a tremendous moment, for there he stood, the heir of the great old Spanish poets, the magnificent Herrera, the nostalgic and moving Fray Luis, Juan de la Cruz, the mystic, and the crabbed and obscure Gongora. He was the last of that long line and he trod in their steps not unworthily. Strangely in my heart sang the lovely and tender song which is the most famous of Don Calisto's lyrics.

I was abashed. It was fortunate for me that I had prepared beforehand the phrase with which I meant to greet him.

"It is a wonderful honour, Maestro, for a foreigner such as I to make the acquaintance of so great a poet."

A flicker of amusement passed through those piercing eyes and a smile for an instant curved the lines of that stern mouth.

"I am not a poet, señor, but a bristle merchant. You have made a mistake, Don Calisto lives next door."

I had come to the wrong house.

# LOUISE

I COULD NEVER UNDERSTAND why Louise bothered with me. She disliked me and I knew that behind my back, in that gentle way of hers, she seldom lost the opportunity of saying a disagreeable thing about me. She had too much delicacy ever to make a direct statement, but with a hint and a sigh and a little flutter of her beautiful hands she was able to make her meaning plain. She was a mistress of cold praise. It was true that we had known one another, almost intimately, for five and twenty years, but it was impossible for me to believe that she could be affected by the claims of old association. She thought me a coarse, brutal, cynical and vulgar fellow. I was puzzled at her not taking the obvious course and dropping me. She did nothing of the kind; indeed, she would not leave me alone; she was constantly asking me to lunch and dine with her and once or twice a year invited me to spend a week-end at her house in the country. At last I thought that I had discovered her motive. She had an uneasy suspicion that I did not believe in her; and if that was why she did not like me, it was also why she sought my acquaintance: it galled her that I alone should look upon her as a comic figure and she could not rest till I acknowledged myself mistaken and defeated. Perhaps she had an inkling that I saw the face behind the mask and because I alone held out was determined that sooner or later I too should take the mask for the face. I was never quite certain that she was a complete humbug. I wondered whether she fooled herself as thoroughly as she fooled the world or whether there was some spark of humour at the bottom of her heart. If there was it might be that she was attracted to me, as a pair of crooks might be attracted to one another, by the knowledge that we shared a secret that was hidden from everybody else.

I knew Louise before she married. She was then a frail, delicate girl with large and melancholy eyes. Her father and mother worshipped her with an anxious adoration, for some illness, scarlet fever I think, had left her with a weak heart and she had to take the greatest care of herself. When Tom Maitland proposed to her they were dismayed, for they were convinced that she was much too delicate for the strenuous state of marriage. But they were not too well off and Tom Maitland was rich. He promised to do everything in the world for Louise and finally they entrusted her to him as a sacred charge. Tom Maitland was a big, husky fellow, very good-looking and a fine athlete. He doted on Louise. With her weak heart he could not hope to keep her with him long and he made up his mind to do everything he could to make her few years on earth happy. He gave up the games he excelled in, not because she wished him to, she was glad that he should play golf and hunt, but because by a coincidence she had a heart attack whenever he proposed to leave her for a day. If they had a difference of opinion she gave in to him at once, for she was the most submissive wife a man could have, but her heart failed her and she would be laid up, sweet and uncomplaining, for a week. He could not be such a brute as to cross her. Then they would have quite a little tussle about which should yield and it was only with difficulty that at last he persuaded her to have her own way. On one occasion seeing her walk eight miles on an expedition that she particularly wanted to make, I suggested to Tom Maitland that she was stronger than one would have thought. He shook his head and sighed.

"No, no, she's dreadfully delicate. She's been to the best heart specialists in the world and they all say that her life hangs on a thread. But she has an unconquerable spirit."

He told her that I had remarked on her endurance.

"I shall pay for it tomorrow," she said to me in her plaintive way. "I shall be at death's door."

"I sometimes think that you're quite strong enough to do the things you want to," I murmured.

I had noticed that if a party was amusing she could dance till five in the morning, but if it was dull she felt very poorly and Tom had to take her home early. I am afraid she did not like my reply, for though she gave me a pathetic little smile I saw no amusement in her large blue eyes.

"You can't very well expect me to fall down dead just to please you," she answered.

Louise outlived her husband. He caught his death of cold one day when they were sailing and Louise needed all the rugs there were to keep her warm. He left her a comfortable fortune and a daughter. Louise was inconsolable. It was wonderful that she managed to survive the shock. Her friends expected her speedily to follow poor Tom Maitland to the grave. Indeed they already felt dreadfully sorry for Iris, her daughter, who would be left an orphan. They redoubled their attentions towards Louise. They would not let her stir a finger; they insisted on doing everything in the world to save her trouble. They had to, because if she was called upon to do anything tiresome or inconvenient her heart went back on her and there she was at death's door. She was entirely lost without a man to take care of her, she said, and she did not know how, with her delicate health, she was going to bring up her dear Iris. Her friends asked why she did not marry again. Oh, with her heart it was out of the question, though of course she knew that dear Tom would have wished her to, and perhaps it would be the best thing for Iris if she did; but who would want to be bothered with a wretched invalid like herself? Oddly enough more than one young man showed himself quite ready to undertake the charge and a year after Tom's death she allowed George Hobhouse to lead her to the altar. He was a fine, upstanding fellow and he was not at all badly off. I never saw anyone so grateful as he for the privilege of being allowed to take care of this frail little thing.

"I shan't live to trouble you long," she said.

He was a soldier and an ambitious one, but he resigned his commission. Louise's health forced her to spend the winter at Monte Carlo and the summer at Deauville. He hesitated a little at throwing up his career, and Louise at first would not hear of it; but at last she yielded as she always yielded, and he prepared to make his wife's last few years as happy as might be.

"It can't be very long now," she said. "I'll try not to be troublesome."

For the next two or three years Louise managed, notwithstanding her weak heart, to go beautifully dressed to all the most lively parties, to gamble very heavily, to dance and even to flirt with tall slim young men. But George Hobhouse had not the stamina of Louise's first husband and he had to brace himself now and then with a stiff drink for his day's work as Louise's second husband. It is possible that the habit would have grown on him, which Louise would not have liked at all, but very fortunately (for her) the war broke out. He rejoined his regiment and three months later was killed. It was a great shock to Louise. She felt, however, that in such a crisis she must not give way to a private grief; and if she had a heart attack nobody heard of it. In order to distract her mind she turned her villa at Monte Carlo into a hospital for convalescent officers. Her friends told her that she would never survive the strain.

"Of course it will kill me," she said, "I know that. But what does it matter? I must do my bit."

It didn't kill her. She had the time of her life. There was no convalescent home in France that was more popular. I met her by chance in Paris. She was lunching at the Ritz with a tall and very handsome young Frenchman. She explained that she was there on business connected with the hospital. She told me that the officers were too charming to her. They knew how delicate she was and they wouldn't let her do a single thing. They took care of her, well—as though they were all her husbands. She sighed.

"Poor George, who would ever have thought that I with my heart should survive him?"

"And poor Tom!" I said.

I don't know why she didn't like my saying that. She gave me her plaintive smile and her beautiful eyes filled with tears.

"You always speak as though you grudged me the few years that I can expect to live."

"By the way, your heart's much better, isn't it?"

"It'll never be better. I saw a specialist this morning and he said I must be prepared for the worst."

"Oh, well, you've been prepared for that for nearly twenty years now, haven't you?"

When the war came to an end Louise settled in London. She was now a woman of over forty, thin and frail still, with large eyes and pale cheeks, but she did not look a day more than twenty-five. Iris, who had been at school and was now grown up, came to live with her.

"She'll take care of me," said Louise. "Of course it'll be hard on her to live with such a great invalid as I am, but it can only be for such a little while, I'm sure she won't mind."

Iris was a nice girl. She had been brought up with the knowledge that her mother's health was precarious. As a child she had never been allowed to make a noise. She had always realized that her mother must on no account be upset. And though Louise told her now that she wouldn't hear of her sacrificing herself for a tiresome old woman the girl simply would not listen. It wasn't a question of sacrificing herself, it was a happiness to do what she could for her poor dear mother. With a sigh her mother let her do a great deal.

"It pleases the child to think she's making herself useful," she said.

"Don't you think she ought to go out and about more?" I asked.

"That's what I'm always telling her. I can't get her to enjoy herself. Heaven knows, I never want anyone to put themselves out on my account."

And Iris, when I remonstrated with her, said: "Poor dear mother, she wants me to go and stay with friends and go to parties, but the moment I start off anywhere she has one of her heart attacks, so I much prefer to stay at home."

But presently she fell in love. A young friend of mine, a very good lad, asked her to marry him and she consented. I liked the child and was glad that she was to be given at last the chance to lead a life of her own. She had never seemed to suspect that such a thing was possible. But one day the young man came to me in great distress and told me that his marriage was indefinitely postponed. Iris felt that she could not desert her mother. Of course it was really no business of mine, but I made the opportunity to go and see Louise. She was always glad to receive her friends at tea-time and now that she was older she cultivated the society of painters and writers.

"Well, I hear that Iris isn't going to be married," I said after a little.

"I don't know about that. She's not going to be married quite so soon as I could have wished. I've begged her on my bended knees not to consider me, but she absolutely refuses to leave me."

"Don't you think it's rather hard on her?"

"Dreadfully. Of course it can only be for a few months, but I hate the thought of anyone sacrificing themselves for me."

"My dear Louise, you've buried two husbands, I can't see the least reason why you shouldn't bury at least two more."

"Do you think that's funny?" she asked me in a tone that she made as offensive as she could.

"I suppose it's never struck you as strange that you're always strong enough to do anything you want to and that your weak heart only prevents you from doing things that bore you?"

"Oh, I know, I know what you've always thought of me. You've never believed that I had anything the matter with me, have you?"

I looked at her full and square.

"Never. I think you've carried out for twenty-five years a stupendous bluff. I think you're the most selfish and monstrous woman I have ever known. You ruined the lives of those two wretched men you married and now you're going to ruin the life of your daughter."

I should not have been surprised if Louise had had a heart attack then. I fully expected her to fly into a passion. She merely gave me a gentle smile.

"My poor friend, one of these days you'll be so dreadfully sorry you said this to me."

"Have you quite determined that Iris shall not marry this boy?"

"I've begged her to marry him. I know it'll kill me, but I don't mind. Nobody cares for me. I'm just a burden to everybody."

"Did you tell her it would kill you?"

"She made me."

"As if anyone ever made you do anything that you were not yourself quite determined to do."

"She can marry her young man tomorrow if she likes. If it kills me, it kills me."

"Well, let's risk it, shall we?"

"Haven't you got any compassion for me?"

"One can't pity anyone who amuses one as much as you amuse me," I answered.

A faint spot of colour appeared on Louise's pale cheeks and though she smiled still her eyes were hard and angry.

"Iris shall marry in a month's time," she said, "and if anything happens to me I hope you and she will be able to forgive yourselves."

Louise was as good as her word. A date was fixed, a trousseau of great magnificence was ordered, and invitations were issued. Iris and the very good lad were radiant. On the wedding day, at ten o'clock in the morning, Louise, that devilish woman, had one of her heart attacks—and died. She died gently forgiving Iris for having killed her.

# THE CLOSED SHOP

NOTHING WOULD INDUCE ME to tell the name of the happy country in which the events occurred that I am constrained to relate; but I see no harm in admitting that it is a free and independent state on the continent of America. This is vague enough in all conscience and can give rise to no diplomatic incident. Now the president of this free and independent state had an eye to a pretty woman and there came to his capital, a wide and sunny town with a plaza, a cathedral that was not without dignity and a few old Spanish houses, a young person from Michigan of such a pleasing aspect that his heart went out to her. He lost no time in declaring his passion and was gratified to learn that it was returned, but he was mortified to discover that the young person regarded his possession of a wife and her possession of a husband as a bar to their union. She had a feminine weakness for marriage. Though it seemed unreasonable to the president, he was not the man to refuse a pretty woman the gratification of her whim and promised to make such arrangements as would enable him to offer her wedlock. He called his attorneys together and put the matter before them. He had long thought, he said, that for a progressive country their marriage laws were remarkably out of date and he proposed therefore radically to amend them. The attorneys retired and after a brief interval devised a divorce law that was satisfactory to the president. But the state of which I write was always careful to do things in a constitutional way, for it was a highly civilized, democratic and reputable country. A president who respects himself and his oath of office cannot promulgate a law, even if it is to his own interest, without adhering to certain forms, and these things take time; the president had barely signed the decree that made the new divorce law valid when a revolution broke out and he was very unfortunately hanged on a lamppost in the plaza in front of the cathedral that was not without dignity. The young person of pleasing aspect left town in a hurry, but the law remained. Its terms were simple. On the payment of one hundred dollars gold and after a residence of thirty days a man could divorce his wife or a wife her husband without even apprising the other party of the intended step. Your wife might tell you that she was going to spend a month with her aged mother and one morning at breakfast when you looked through your mail you might receive a letter from her informing you that she had divorced you and was already married to another.

Now it was not long before the happy news spread here and there that at a reasonable distance from New York was a country, the capital of which had an equable climate and tolerable accommodation, where a woman could release herself, expeditiously and with economy, from the irksome bonds of matrimony. The fact that the operation could be performed without the husband's knowledge saved her from those preliminary and acrimonious discussions that are so wearing to the nerves. Every woman knows that however much a man may argue about a proposition he will generally accept a fact with resignation. Tell him you want a Rolls-Royce and he will say he can't afford it, but buy it and he will sign his cheque like a lamb. So in a very short time beautiful women in considerable numbers began to come down to the pleasant, sunny town; tired business women and women of fashion, women of pleasure and women of leisure; they came from New York, Chicago and San Francisco, they came from Georgia and they came from Dakota, they came from all the states in the Union. The passenger accommodation on the ships of the United Fruit Line was only just adequate to the demand, and if you wanted a stateroom to yourself you had to engage it six months in advance. Prosperity descended upon the capital of this enterprising state and in a very little while there was not a lawyer in it who did not own a Ford car. Don Agosto, the proprietor of the Grand Hotel, went to the expense of building several bathrooms, but he did not grudge it; he was making a fortune, and he never passed the lamp-post on which the outgoing president had been hanged without giving it a jaunty wave of his hand.

"He was a great man," he said. "One day they will erect a statue to him."

I have spoken as though it were only women who availed themselves of this convenient and reasonable law, and this might indicate that in the United States it is they rather than men who desire release from the impediment of Holy Matrimony. I have no reason to believe that this is so. Though it was women in great majority who travelled to this country to get a divorce, I ascribe this to the fact that it is always easy for them to get away for six weeks (a week there, a week back and thirty days to establish a domicile) but it is difficult for men to leave their affairs so long. It is true that they could go there during their summer holidays, but then the heat is somewhat oppressive; and besides, there are no golf links: it is reasonable enough to suppose that many a man will hesitate to divorce his wife when he can only do it at the cost of a month's golf. There were of course two or three males spending their thirty days at the Grand Hotel, but they were generally, for a reason that is obscure, commercial travellers. I can but imagine that by the nature of their avocations they were able at one and the same time to pursue freedom and profit.

Be this as it may, the fact remains that the inmates of the Grand Hotel were for the most part women, and very gay it was in the patio at luncheon and at dinner when they sat at little square tables under the arches, discussing their matrimonial troubles and drinking champagne. Don Agosto did a roaring trade with the generals and colonels (there were more generals than colonels in the army of this state), the lawyers, bankers, merchants, and the young sparks of the town who came to look at these beautiful creatures. But the perfect is seldom realized in this world. There is always something that is not quite right and women engaged in getting rid of their husbands are very properly in an agitated condition. It makes them at times hard to please. Now it must be confessed that this delightful little city, notwithstanding its manifold advantages, somewhat lacked places of amusement. There was but one cinema and this showed films that had been wandering too long from their happy home in

Hollywood. In the daytime you could have consultations with your lawyer, polish your nails and do a little shopping, but the evenings were intolerable. There were many complaints that thirty days was a long time and more than one impatient young thing asked her lawyer why they didn't put a little pep into their law and do the whole job in eight and forty hours. Don Agosto, however, was a man of resource and presently he had an inspiration: he engaged a troupe of wandering Guatemaltecans who played the marimba. There is no music in the world that sets the toes so irresistibly tingling and in a little while everyone in the patio began dancing. It is of course obvious that twenty-five beautiful women cannot dance with three commercial travellers, but there were all these generals and colonels and there were all the young sparks of the town. They danced divinely and they had great liquid black eyes. The hours flew, the days tripped one upon the heels of the other so quickly that the month passed before you realized it, and more than one of Don Agosto's guests when she bade him farewell confessed that she would willingly have stayed longer. Don Agosto was radiant. He liked to see people enjoy themselves. The marimba band was worth twice the money he paid for it, and it did his heart good to see his ladies dance with the gallant officers and the young men of the town. Since Don Agosto was thrifty he always turned off the electric light on the stairs and in the passages at ten o'clock at night and the gallant officers and the young men of the town improved their English wonderfully.

Everything went as merrily as a marriage bell, if I may use a phrase that, however hackneyed, in this connection is irresistible, till one day Madame Coralie came to the conclusion that she had had enough of it. For one man's meat is another man's poison. She dressed herself and went to call on her friend Carmencita. After she had in a few voluble words stated the purpose of her visit Carmencita called a maid and told her to run and fetch La Gorda. They had a matter of importance which they wished to discuss with her. La Gorda, a woman of ample proportions with a heavy moustache, soon joined them and over a bottle of malaga the three of them held a momentous conversation. The result of it was that they indited a letter to the president asking for an audience. The new president was a hefty young man in the early thirties who a few years before had been a stevedore in the employment of an American firm, and he had risen to his present exalted station by a natural eloquence and an effective use of his gun when he wanted to make a point or emphasize a statement. When one of his secretaries placed the letter before him he laughed.

"What do those three old faggots want with me?"

But he was a good-natured fellow and accessible. He did not forget that he had been elected by the people, as one of the people, to protect the people. He had also during his early youth been employed for some months by Madame Coralie to run errands. He told his secretary that he would see them at ten o'clock next morning. They went at the appointed hour to the palace and were led up a noble stairway to the audience chamber; the official who conducted them knocked softly on the door; a barred judas was opened and a suspicious eye appeared. The president had no intention of suffering the fate of his predecessor if he could help it and no matter who his visitors were did not receive them without precaution. The official gave the three ladies' names, the door was opened, but not too wide, and they slipped in. It was a handsome room and various secretaries at little tables, in their shirt sleeves and with a revolver on each hip, were busy typing. One or two other young men, heavily armed, were lying on sofas reading the papers and smoking cigarettes. The president, also in his shirt sleeves, with a revolver in his belt, was standing with his thumbs in the sleeve holes of his waistcoat. He was tall and stout, of a handsome and even dignified presence.

"Qué tal?" he cried jovially, with a flash of his white teeth. "What brings you here, señoras?"

"How well you're looking, Don Manuel," said La Gorda. "You are a fine figure of a man."

He shook hands with them, and his staff, ceasing their strenuous activity, leaned back and cordially waved their hands to the three ladies. They were old friends and the greetings, if a trifle sardonic, were hearty. I must disclose the fact now (which I could without doubt do in a manner so discreet that I might be misunderstood; but if you have to say something you may just as well say it plainly as not) that these three ladies were the madams of the three principal brothels in the capital of this free and independent state. La Gorda and Carmencita were of Spanish origin and were very decently dressed in black, with black silk shawls over their heads, but Madame Coralie was French and she wore a toque. They were all of mature age and of modest demeanour.

The president made them sit down and offered them madeira and cigarettes, but they refused.

"No, thank you, Don Manuel," said Madame Coralie. "It is on business that we have come to see you."

"Well, what can I do for you?"

La Gorda and Carmencita looked at Madame Coralie and Madame Coralie looked at La Gorda and Carmencita. They nodded and she saw that they expected her to be their spokeswoman.

"Well, Don Manuel, it is like this. We are three women who have worked hard for many years and not a breath of scandal has ever tarnished our good names. There are not in all the Americas three more distinguished houses than ours and they are a credit to this beautiful city. Why, only last year I spent five hundred dollars to supply my sala principal with plate-glass mirrors. We have always been respectable and we have paid our taxes with regularity. It is hard now that the fruits of our labours should be snatched away from us. I do not hesitate to say that after so many years of honest and conscientious attention to business it is unjust that we should have to submit to such treatment."

The president was astounded.

"But, Coralie, my dear, I do not know what you mean. Has anyone dared to claim money from you that the law does not sanction or that I know nothing about?"

He gave his secretaries a suspicious glance. They tried to look innocent, but though they were, only succeeded in looking uneasy.

"It is the law we complain of. Ruin stares us in the face."

"Ruin?"

"So long as this new divorce law is in existence we can do no business and we may just as well shut up our beautiful houses."

Then Madame Coralie explained in a manner so frank that I prefer to paraphrase her speech that owing to this invasion of the town by beautiful ladies from a foreign land the three elegant houses on which she and her two friends paid rates and taxes were utterly deserted. The young men of fashion preferred to spend their evenings at the Grand Hotel where they received for soft words entertainment which at the regular establishments they could only have got for hard cash.

"You cannot blame them," said the president.

"I don't," cried Madame Coralie. "I blame the women. They have no right to come and take the bread out of our mouths. Don Manuel, you are one of the people, you are not one of these aristocrats: what will the country say if you allow us to be driven out of business by blacklegs? I ask you is it just, is it honest?"

"But what can I do?" said the president. "I cannot lock them up in their rooms for thirty days. How am I to blame if these foreigners have no sense of decency?"

"It's different for a poor girl," said La Gorda. "She has her way to make. But that these women do that sort of thing when they're not obliged to, no, that I shall never understand."

"It is a bad and wicked law," said Carmencita.

The president sprang to his feet and threw his arms akimbo.

"You are not going to ask me to abrogate a law that has brought peace and plenty to this country. I am of the people and I was elected by the people, and the prosperity of my fatherland is very near my heart. Divorce is our staple industry and the law shall be repealed only over my dead body."

"Oh, Maria Santissima, that it should come to this," said Carmencita. "And me with two daughters in a convent in New Orleans. Ah, in this business one often has unpleasantness, but I always consoled myself by thinking that my daughters would marry well, and when the time came for me to retire they would inherit my business. Do you think I can keep them in a convent in New Orleans for nothing?"

"And who is going to keep my son at Harvard if I have to close my house, Don Manuel?" asked La Gorda.

"As for myself," said Madame Coralie, "I do not care. I shall return to France. My dear mother is eighty-seven years of age and she cannot live very much longer. It will be a comfort to her if I spend her last remaining years by her side. But it is the injustice of it that hurts. You have spent many happy evenings in my house, Don Manuel, and I am wounded that you should let us be treated like this. Did you not tell me yourself that it was the proudest day of your life when you entered as an honoured guest the house in which you had once been employed as errand boy?"

"I do not deny it. I stood champagne all round." Don Manuel walked up and down the large hall, shrugging his shoulders as he went, and now and then, deep in thought, he gesticulated. "I am of the people, elected by the people," he cried, "and the fact is, these women are blacklegs." He turned to his secretaries with a dramatic gesture. "It is a stain on my administration. It is against all my principles to allow unskilled foreign labour to take the bread out of the mouths of honest and industrious people. These ladies are quite right to come to me and appeal for my protection. I will not allow the scandal to continue."

It was of course a pointed and effective speech, but all who heard it knew that it left things exactly where they were. Madame Coralie powdered her nose and gave it, a commanding organ, a brief look in her pocket mirror.

"Of course I know what human nature is," she said, "and I can well understand that time hangs heavily on the hands of these creatures."

"We could build a golf course," hazarded one of the secretaries. "It is true that this would only occupy them by day."

"If they want men why can't they bring them with them?" said La Gorda.

"Caramba!" cried the president and with that stood on a sudden quite still. "There is the solution."

He had not reached his exalted station without being a man of insight and resource. He beamed.

"We will amend the law. Men shall come in as before without let or hindrance, but women only accompanied by their husbands or with their written consent." He saw the look of consternation which his secretaries gave him, and he waved his hand. "But the immigration authorities shall receive instructions to interpret the word husband with the widest latitude."

"Maria Santissima!" cried Madame Coralie. "If they come with a friend he will take care that no one else interferes with them and our customers will return to the houses where for so long they have been so hospitably entertained. Don Manuel, you are a great man and one of these days they will erect a statue to you."

It is often the simplest expedients that settle the most formidable difficulties. The law was briefly amended according to the terms of Don Manuel's suggestion, and whereas prosperity continued to pour its blessings on the wide and sunny capital of this free and independent state, Madame Coralie was enabled profitably to pursue her useful avocations, Carmencita's two daughters completed their expensive education in the convent at New Orleans and La Gorda's son successfully graduated at Harvard.

# THE PROMISE

My wife is a very unpunctual woman, so when, having arranged to lunch with her at Claridge's, I arrived there ten minutes late and did not find her I was not surprised. I ordered a cocktail. It was the height of the season and there were but two or three vacant tables in the lounge. Some of the people after an early meal were drinking their coffee, others like myself were toying with a dry martini; the women in their summer frocks looked gay and charming and the men debonair; but I could see no one whose appearance sufficiently interested me to occupy the quarter of an hour I was expecting to wait. They were slim and pleasant to look upon, well dressed and carelessly at ease, but they were for the most part of a pattern and I observed them with tolerance rather than with curiosity. But it was two o'clock and I felt hungry. My wife tells me that she can neither wear a turquoise nor a watch, for the turquoise turns green and the watch stops; and this she attributes to the malignity of fate. I have nothing to say about the turquoise, but I sometimes think the watch might go if she wound it. I was engaged with these reflections when an attendant came up and with that hushed significance that hotel attendants affect (as though their message held a more sinister meaning than their words suggested) told me that a lady had just telephoned to say that she had been detained and could not lunch with me.

I hesitated. It is not very amusing to eat in a crowded restaurant by oneself, but it was late to go to a club and I decided that I had better stay where I was. I strolled into the dining-room. It has never given me any particular satisfaction (as it appears to do to so many elegant persons) to be known by name to the headwaiters of fashionable restaurants, but on this occasion I should certainly have been glad to be greeted by less stony an eye. The maître d'hôtel with a set and hostile face told me that every table was occupied. I looked helplessly round the large and stately room and on a sudden to my pleasure caught sight of someone I knew. Lady Elizabeth Vermont was an old friend. She smiled and noticing that she was alone I went up to her.

"Will you take pity on a hungry man and let me sit with you?" I asked.

"Oh, do. But I've nearly finished."

She was at a little table by the side of a massive column and when I took my place I found that notwithstanding the crowd we sat almost in privacy.

"This is a bit of luck for me," I said. "I was on the point of fainting from hunger."

She had a very agreeable smile; it did not light up her face suddenly, but seemed rather to suffuse it by degrees with charm. It hesitated for a moment about her lips and then slowly travelled to those great shining eyes of hers and there softly lingered. No one surely could say that Elizabeth Vermont was cast in the common mould. I never knew her when she was a girl, but many have told me that then she was so lovely, it brought the tears to one's eyes, and I could well believe it; for now, though fifty, she was still incomparable. Her ravaged beauty made the fresh and blooming comeliness of youth a trifle insipid. I do not like these painted faces that look all alike; and I think women are foolish to dull their expression and obscure their personality with powder, rouge and lipstick. But Elizabeth Vermont painted not to imitate nature, but to improve it; you did not question the means but applauded the result. The flaunting boldness with which she used cosmetics increased rather than diminished the character of that perfect face. I suppose her hair was dyed; it was black and sleek and shining. She held herself upright as though she had never learned to loll and she was very slim. She wore a dress of black satin, the lines and simplicity of which were admirable, and about her neck was a long rope of pearls. Her only other jewel was an enormous emerald which guarded her wedding ring, and its sombre fire emphasized the whiteness of her hand. But it was in her hands with their reddened nails that she most clearly betrayed her age; they had none of a girl's soft and dimpled roundness; and you could not but look at them with a certain dismay. Before very long they would look like the talons of a bird of prey.

Elizabeth Vermont was a remarkable woman. Of great birth, for she was the daughter of the seventh Duke of St Erth, she married at the age of eighteen a very rich man and started at once upon a career of astounding extravagance, lewdness and dissipation. She was too proud to be cautious, too reckless to think of consequences, and within two years her husband in circumstances of appalling scandal divorced her. She married then one of the three co-respondents named in the case and eighteen months later ran away from him. Then followed a succession of lovers. She became notorious for her profligacy. Her startling beauty and her outrageous conduct held her in the public eye and it was never very long but that she gave the gossips something to talk about. Her name stank in the nostrils of decent people. She was a gambler, a spendthrift and a wanton. But though unfaithful to her lovers she was constant to her friends and there always remained a few who would never allow, whatever she did, that she was anything but a very nice woman. She had candour, high spirits and courage. She was never a hypocrite. She was generous and sincere. It was at this period of her life that I came to know her; for great ladies, now that religion is out of fashion, when they are very much blown upon take a flattering interest in the arts. When they receive the cold shoulder from members of their own class they condescend sometimes to the society of writers, painters and musicians. I found her an agreeable companion. She was one of those blessed persons who say quite fearlessly what they think (thus saving much useful time) and she had a ready wit. She was always willing to talk (with a diverting humour) of her lurid past. Her conversation, though uninstructed, was good, because, notwithstanding everything, she was an honest woman.

Then she did a very surprising thing. At the age of forty she married a boy of twenty-one. Her friends said it was the maddest act of all her life, and some who had stuck to her through thick and thin, now for the boy's sake, because he was nice and it seemed dreadful thus to take advantage of his inexperience, refused to have anything more to do with her. It really was the limit. They prophesied disaster, for Elizabeth Vermont was incapable of sticking to any man for more than six months, nay, they hoped for it, since it seemed the only chance for the wretched youth that his wife should behave so shamelessly that he must leave her. They were all wrong. I do not know whether time was responsible for a change of heart in her, or whether Peter Vermont's innocence and simple love touched her, but the fact remains that she made him an admirable wife. They were poor, and she was extravagant, but she became a thrifty housewife; she grew on a sudden so careful of her reputation that the tongue of scandal was silenced. His happiness seemed her only concern. No one could doubt that she loved him devotedly. After being the subject of so much conversation for so long Elizabeth Vermont ceased to be talked about. It looked as though her story were told. She was a changed woman, and I amused myself with the notion that when she was a very old lady, with many years of perfect respectability behind her, the past, the lurid past, would seem to belong not to her but to someone long since dead whom once she had vaguely known. For women have an enviable faculty of forgetting.

But who can tell what the fates have in store? In the twinkling of an eye all was changed. Peter Vermont, after ten years of an ideal marriage, fell madly in love with a girl called Barbara Canton. She was a nice girl, the youngest daughter of Lord Robert Canton who was at one time Under Secretary for Foreign Affairs, and she was pretty in a fair and fluffy way. Of course she was not for a moment to be compared with Lady Elizabeth. Many people knew what had happened, but no one could tell whether Elizabeth Vermont had any inkling of it, and they wondered how she would meet a situation that was so foreign to her experience. It was always she who had discarded her lovers; none had deserted her. For my part I thought she would make short work of little Miss Canton; I knew her courage and her adroitness. All this was in my mind now while we chatted over our luncheon. There was nothing in her demeanour, as gay, charming and frank as usual, to suggest that anything troubled her. She talked as she always talked, lightly but with good sense and a lively perception of the ridiculous, of the various topics which the course of conversation brought forward. I enjoyed myself. I came to the conclusion that by some miracle she had no notion of Peter's changed feelings and I explained this to myself by the supposition that her love for him was so great, she could not conceive that his for her might be less.

We drank our coffee and smoked a couple of cigarettes and she asked me the time.

"A quarter to three."

"I must ask for my bill."

"Won't you let me stand you lunch?"

"Of course," she smiled.

"Are you in a hurry?"

"I'm meeting Peter at three."

"Oh, how is he?"

"He's very well."

She gave a little smile, that tardy and delightful smile of hers, but I seemed to discern in it a certain mockery. For an instant she hesitated and she looked at me with deliberation.

"You like curious situations, don't you?" she said. "You'd never guess the errand I'm bound on. I rang up Peter this morning and asked him to meet me at three. I'm going to ask him to divorce me."

"You're not," I cried. I felt myself flush and did not know what to say. "I thought you got on so well together."

"Do you think it's likely that I shouldn't know what all the world knows? I'm really not such a fool as all that."

She was not a woman to whom it was possible to say what one did not believe and I could not pretend that I did not know what she meant. I remained silent for a second or two.

"Why should you allow yourself to be divorced?"

"Robert Canton is a stuffy old thing. I very much doubt if he'd let Barbara marry Peter if I divorced him. And for me, you know, it isn't of the smallest consequence: one divorce more or less . . ."

She shrugged her pretty shoulders.

"How do you know he wants to marry her?"

"He's head over ears in love with her."

"Has he told you so?"

"No. He doesn't even know that I know. He's been so wretched, poor darling. He's been trying so hard not to hurt my feelings."

"Perhaps it's only a momentary infatuation," I hazarded. "It may pass."

"Why should it? Barbara's young and pretty. She's quite nice. They're very well suited to one another. And besides, what good would it do if it did pass? They love each other now and the present in love is all that matters. I'm nineteen years older than Peter. If a man stops loving a woman old enough to be his mother do you think he'll ever come to love her again? You're a novelist, you must know more about human nature than that."

"Why should you make this sacrifice?"

"When he asked me to marry him ten years ago I promised him that when he wanted his release he should have it. You see, there was so great a disproportion between our ages I thought that was only fair."

"And are you going to keep a promise that he hasn't asked you to keep?"

She gave a little flutter of those long thin hands of hers and now I felt that there was something ominous in the dark glitter of that emerald.

"Oh, I must, you know. One must behave like a gentleman. To tell you the truth that's why I'm lunching here today. It was at this table that he proposed to me; we were dining together, you know, and I was sitting just where I am now. The nuisance is that I'm just as much in love with him now as I was then." She paused for a minute and I could see that she clenched her teeth. "Well, I suppose I ought to go. Peter hates one to keep him waiting."

She gave me a sort of little helpless look and it struck me that she simply could not bring herself to rise from her chair. But she smiled and with an abrupt gesture sprang to her feet.

"Would you like me to come with you?"

"As far as the hotel door," she smiled.

We walked through the restaurant and the lounge and when we came to the entrance a porter swung round the revolving doors. I asked if she would like a taxi.

"No, I'd sooner walk, it's such a lovely day." She

gave me her hand. "It's been so nice to see you. I shall go abroad tomorrow, but I expect to be in London all the autumn. Do ring me up."

She smiled and nodded and turned away. I watched her walk up Davies Street. The air was still bland and springlike and above the roofs little white clouds were sailing leisurely in a blue sky. She held herself very erect and the poise of her head was gallant. She was a slim and lovely figure so that people looked at her as they passed. I saw her bow graciously to some acquaintance who raised his hat, and I thought that never in a thousand years would it occur to him that she had a breaking heart. I repeat, she was a very honest woman.

# A STRING OF BEADS

"WHAT A BIT OF LUCK that I'm placed next to you," said Laura, as we sat down to dinner.

"For me," I replied politely.

"That remains to be seen. I particularly wanted to have the chance of talking to you. I've got a story to tell you."

At this my heart sank a little.

"I'd sooner you talked about yourself," I answered. "Or even about me."

"Oh, but I must tell you the story. I think you'll be able to use it."

"If you must, you must. But let's look at the menu first."

"Don't you want me to?" she said, somewhat aggrieved. "I thought you'd be pleased."

"I am. You might have written a play and wanted to read me that."

"It happened to some friends of mine. It's perfectly true."

"That's no recommendation. A true story is never quite so true as an invented one."

"What does that mean?"

"Nothing very much," I admitted. "But I thought it sounded well."

"I wish you'd let me get on with it."

"I'm all attention. I'm not going to eat the soup. It's fattening."

She gave me a pinched look and then glanced at the menu. She uttered a little sigh.

"Oh, well, if you're going to deny yourself I suppose I must too. Heaven knows, I can't afford to take liberties with my figure."

"And yet is there any soup more heavenly than the sort of soup in which you put a great dollop of cream?"

"Bortsch," she sighed. "It's the only soup I really like."

"Never mind. Tell me your story and we'll forget about food till the fish comes."

"Well, I was actually there when it happened. I was dining with the Livingstones. Do you know the Livingstones?"

"No, I don't think I do."

"Well, you can ask them and they'll confirm every word I say. They'd asked their governess to come in to dinner because some woman had thrown them over at the last moment—you know how inconsiderate people are—and they would have been thirteen at table. Their governess was a Miss Robinson, quite a nice girl, young, you know, twenty or twenty-one, and rather pretty. Personally I would never engage a governess who was young and pretty. One never knows."

"But one hopes for the best."

Laura paid no attention to my remark.

"The chances are that she'll be thinking of young men instead of attending to her duties and then, just when she's got used to your ways, she'll want to go and get married. But Miss Robinson had excellent references, and I must allow that she was a very nice, respectable person. I believe in point of fact she was a clergyman's daughter.

"There was a man at dinner whom I don't suppose you've ever heard of, but who's quite a celebrity in his way. He's a Count Borselli and he knows more about precious stones than anyone in the world. He was sitting next to Mary Lyngate, who rather fancies herself on her pearls, and in the course of conversation she asked him what he thought of the string she was wearing. He said it was very pretty. She was rather piqued at this and told him it was valued at eight thousand pounds.

" 'Yes, it's worth that,' he said.

"Miss Robinson was sitting opposite to him. She was looking rather nice that evening. Of course I recognized her dress, it was one of Sophie's old ones; but if you hadn't known Miss Robinson was the governess you would never have suspected it.

" 'That's a very beautiful necklace that young lady has on,' said Borselli.

" 'Oh, but that's Mrs Livingstone's governess,' said Mary Lyngate.

" 'I can't help that,' he said. 'She's wearing one of the finest strings of pearls for its size that I've ever seen in my life. It must be worth fifty thousand pounds.'

" 'Nonsense.'

" 'I give you my word it is.'

"Mary Lyngate leant over. She has rather a shrill voice.

" 'Miss Robinson, do you know what Count Borselli says?' she exclaimed. 'He says that string of pearls you're wearing is worth fifty thousand pounds.'

"Just at that moment there was a sort of pause in the conversation so that everybody heard. We all turned and looked at Miss Robinson. She flushed a little and laughed.

" 'Well, I made a very good bargain,' she said, 'because I paid fifteen shillings for it.'

" 'You certainly did.'

"We all laughed. It was of course absurd. We've all heard of wives palming off on their husbands as false a string of pearls that was real and expensive. That story is as old as the hills."

"Thank you," I said, thinking of a little narrative of my own.

"But it was too ridiculous to suppose that a governess would remain a governess if she owned a string of pearls worth fifty thousand pounds. It was obvious that the Count had made a bloomer. Then an extraordinary thing happened. The long arm of coincidence came in."

"It shouldn't," I retorted. "It's had too much exercise. Haven't you seen that charming book called A Dictionary of English Usage?"

"I wish you wouldn't interrupt just when I'm really getting to the exciting point."

But I had to do so again, for just then a young grilled salmon was insinuated round my left elbow.

"Mrs. Livingstone is giving us a heavenly dinner," I said.

"Is salmon fattening?" asked Laura.

"Very," I answered as I took a large helping.

"Bunk," she said.

"Go on," I begged her. "The long arm of coincidence was about to make a gesture."

"Well, at that very moment the butler bent over Miss Robinson and whispered something in her ear. I thought she turned a trifle pale. It's such a mistake not to wear rouge; you never know what tricks nature will play on you. She certainly looked startled. She leant forwards.

" 'Mrs Livingstone, Dawson says there are two men in the hall who want to speak to me at once.'

" 'Well, you'd better go,' said Sophie Livingstone.

"Miss Robinson got up and left the room. Of course the same thought flashed through all our minds, but I said it first.

" 'I hope they haven't come to arrest her,' I said to Sophie. 'It would be too dreadful for you, my dear.'

" 'Are you sure it was a real necklace, Borselli?' she asked.

" 'Oh, quite.'

" 'She could hardly have had the nerve to wear it tonight if it were stolen,' I said.

"Sophie Livingstone turned as pale as death under her make-up and I saw she was wondering if everything was all right in her jewel case. I only had on a little chain of diamonds, but instinctively I put my hand up to my neck to feel if it was still there.

" 'Don't talk nonsense,' said Mr Livingstone. 'How on earth would Miss Robinson have had the chance of sneaking a valuable string of pearls?'

" 'She may be a receiver,' I said.

" 'Oh, but she had such wonderful references,' said Sophie.

" 'They always do,' I said."

I was positively forced to interrupt Laura once more.

"You don't seem to have been determined to take a very bright view of the case," I remarked.

"Of course I knew nothing against Miss Robinson and I had every reason to think her a very nice girl, but it would have been rather thrilling to find out that she was a notorious thief and a well-known member of a gang of international crooks."

"Just like a film. I'm dreadfully afraid that it's only in films that exciting things like that happen."

"Well, we waited in breathless suspense. There was not a sound. I expected to hear a scuffle in the hall or at least a smothered shriek. I thought the silence very ominous. Then the door opened and Miss Robinson walked in. I noticed at once that the necklace was gone. I could see that she was pale and excited. She came back to the table, sat down and with a smile threw on it——"

"On what?"

"On the table, you fool. A string of pearls."

" 'There's my necklace,' she said.

"Count Borselli leant forwards.

" 'Oh, but those are false,' he said.

" 'I told you they were,' she laughed.

" 'That's not the same string you had on a few moments ago,' he said.

"She shook her head and smiled mysteriously. We were all intrigued. I don't know that Sophie Livingstone was so very much pleased at her governess making herself the centre of interest like that and I thought there was a suspicion of tartness in her manner when she suggested that Miss Robinson had better explain. Well, Miss Robinson said that when she went into the hall she found two men who said they'd come from Jarrot's Stores. She'd bought her string there, as she said, for fifteen shillings, and she'd taken it back because the clasp was loose and had only fetched it that afternoon. The men said they had given her the wrong string. Someone had left a string of real pearls to be restrung and the assistant had made a mistake. Of course I can't understand how anyone could be so stupid as to take a really valuable string to Jarrot's, they aren't used to dealing with that sort of thing, and they wouldn't know real pearls from false; but you know what fools some women are. Anyhow it was the string Miss Robinson was wearing and it was valued at fifty thousand pounds. She naturally gave it back to them—she couldn't do anything else, I suppose, though it must have been a wrench—and they returned her own string to her; then they said that although of course they were under no obligation—you know the silly, pompous way men talk when they're trying to be businesslike—they were instructed, as a solatium or whatever you call it, to offer her a cheque for three hundred pounds. Miss Robinson actually showed it to us. She was as pleased as Punch."

"Well, it was a piece of luck, wasn't it?"

"You'd have thought so. As it turned out it was the ruin of her."

"Oh, how was that?"

"Well, when the time came for her to go on her holiday she told Sophie Livingstone that she'd made up her mind to go to Deauville for a month and blue the whole three hundred pounds. Of course Sophie tried to dissuade her, and begged her to put the money in the savings bank, but she wouldn't hear of it. She said she'd never had such a chance before and would never have it again and she meant for at least four weeks to live like a duchess. Sophie couldn't really do anything and so she gave way. She sold Miss Robinson a lot of clothes that she didn't want; she'd been wearing them all through the season and was sick to death of them; she says she gave them to her, but I don't suppose she quite did that—I dare say she sold them very cheap—

and Miss Robinson started off, entirely alone, for Deauville. What do you think happened then?"

"I haven't a notion," I replied. "I hope she had the time of her life."

"Well, a week before she was due to come back she wrote to Sophie and said that she'd changed her plans and had entered another profession and hoped Mrs Livingstone would forgive her if she didn't return. Of course poor Sophie was furious. What had actually happened was that Miss Robinson had picked up a rich Argentine in Deauville and had gone off to Paris with him. She's been in Paris ever since. I've seen her myself at Florence's, with bracelets right up to her elbow and ropes of pearls round her neck. Of course I cut her dead. They say she has a house in the Bois de Boulogne and I know she has a Rolls. She threw over the Argentine in a few months and then got hold of a Greek; I don't know who she's with now, but the long and short of it is that she's far and away the smartest cocotte in Paris."

"When you say she was ruined you use the word in a purely technical sense, I conclude," said I.

"I don't know what you mean by that," said Laura. "But don't you think you could make a story out of it?"

"Unfortunately I've already written a story about

a pearl necklace. One can't go on writing stories about pearl necklaces."

"I've got half a mind to write it myself. Only of course I should change the end."

"Oh, how would you end it?"

"Well, I should have had her engaged to a bank clerk who had been badly knocked about in the war, with only one leg, say, or half his face shot away; and they'd be dreadfully poor and there would be no prospect of their marriage for years, and he would be putting all his savings into buying a little house in the suburbs and they'd have arranged to marry when he had saved the last instalment. And then she takes him the three hundred pounds and they can hardly believe it, they're so happy, and he cries on her shoulder. He just cries like a child. And they get the little house in the suburbs and they marry, and they have his old mother to live with them, and he goes to the bank every day, and if she's careful not to have babies she can still go out as a daily governess, and he's often ill—with his wound, you know—and she nurses him, and it's all very pathetic and sweet and lovely."

"It sounds rather dull to me," I ventured.

"Yes, but moral," said Laura.

# THE BUM

GOD KNOWS how often I had lamented that I had not half the time I needed to do half the things I wanted. I could not remember when last I had had a moment to myself. I had often amused my fancy with the prospect of just one week's complete idleness. Most of us when not busy working are busy playing; we ride, play tennis or golf, swim or gamble; but I saw myself doing nothing at all. I would lounge through the morning, dawdle through the afternoon and loaf through the evening. My mind would be a slate and each passing hour a sponge that wiped out the scribblings written on it by the world of sense. Time, because it is so fleeting, time, because it is beyond recall, is the most precious of human goods and to squander it is the most delicate form of dissipation in which man can indulge. Cleopatra dissolved in wine a priceless pearl, but she gave it to Anthony to drink; when you waste the brief golden hours you take the beaker in which the gem is melted and dash its contents to the ground. The gesture is grand and like all grand gestures absurd. That of course is its excuse. In the week I promised myself I should naturally read, for to the habitual reader reading is a drug of which he is the slave; deprive him of printed matter and he grows nervous, moody and restless; then, like the alcoholic bereft of brandy who will drink shellac or methylated spirit, he will make do with the advertisements of a paper five years old; he will make do with a telephone directory. But the professional writer is seldom a disinterested reader. I wished my reading to be but another form of idleness. I made up my mind that if ever the happy day arrived when I could enjoy untroubled leisure I would complete an enterprise that had always tempted me, but which hitherto, like an explorer making reconnaissances into an undiscovered country, I had done little more than enter upon: I would read the entire works of Nick Carter.

But I had always fancied myself choosing my moment with surroundings to my liking, not having it forced upon me; and when I was suddenly faced with nothing to do and had to make the best of it (as with a steamship acquaintance whom in the wide waste of the Pacific Ocean you have invited to stay with you in London and who turns up without warning and with all his luggage) I was not a little taken aback. I had come to Vera Cruz from Mexico City to catch one of the Ward Company's white cool ships to Yucatan; and found to my dismay that, a dock strike having been declared overnight, my ship would not put in. I was stuck in Vera Cruz. I took a room in the Hotel Diligencias overlooking the plaza, and spent the morning looking at the sights of the town. I wandered down side streets and peeped into quaint courts. I sauntered through the parish church; it is picturesque with its gargoyles and flying buttresses, and the salt wind and the blazing sun have patined its harsh and massive walls with the mellowness of age; its cupola is covered with white and blue tiles. Then I found that I had seen all that was to be seen and I sat down in the coolness of the arcade that surrounded the square and ordered a drink. The sun beat down on the plaza with a merciless splendour. The coco palms drooped dusty and bedraggled. Great black buzzards perched on them for a moment uneasily, swooped to the ground to gather some bit of offal, and then with lumbering wings flew up to the church tower. I watched the people crossing the square; negroes, Indians, Creoles and Spanish, the motley people of the Spanish Main; and they varied in colour from ebony to ivory. As the morning wore on the tables around me filled up, chiefly with men, who had come to have a drink before luncheon, for the most part in white ducks, but some notwithstanding the heat in the dark clothes of professional respectability. A small band, a guitarist, a blind fiddler and a harpist, played ragtime and after every other tune the guitarist came round with a plate. I had already bought the local paper and I was adamant to the newsvendors who pertinaciously sought to sell me more copies of the same sheet. I refused, oh, twenty times at least, the solicitations of grimy urchins who wanted to shine my spotless shoes; and having come to the end of my small change I could only shake my head at the beggars who importuned me. They gave one no peace. Little Indian women, in shapeless rags, each one with a baby tied in the shawl on her back, held out skinny hands and in a whimper recited a dismal screed; blind men were led up to my table by small boys; the maimed, the halt, the deformed exhibited the sores and the monstrosities with which nature or accident had afflicted them; and half-naked, underfed children whined endlessly their demand for coppers. But these kept their eyes open for the fat policeman who would suddenly dart out on them with a thong and give them a sharp cut on the back or over the head. Then they would scamper, only to return again when, exhausted by the exercise of so much energy, he relapsed into lethargy.

But suddenly my attention was attracted by a beggar who, unlike the rest of them and indeed the people sitting round me, swarthy and black-haired, had hair and beard of a red so vivid that it was startling. His beard was ragged and his long mop of hair looked as though it had not been brushed for months. He wore only a pair of trousers and a cotton singlet, but they were tatters, grimy and foul, that barely held together. I have never seen anyone so thin; his legs, his naked arms, were but skin and bone and through the rents of his singlet you saw every rib of his wasted body; you could count the bones of his dust-covered feet. Of that starveling band he was easily the most abject. He was not old, he could not well have been more than forty, and I could not but ask myself what had brought him to this pass. It was absurd to think that he would not have worked if work he had been able to get. He was the only one of the beggars who did not speak. The rest of them poured forth their litany of woe and if it did not bring the alms they asked continued until an impatient word from you chased them away. He said nothing. I suppose he felt that his look of destitution was all the appeal he needed. He did not even hold out his hand, he merely looked at you, but with such wretchedness in his eyes, such despair in his attitude, it was dreadful; he stood on and on, silent and immobile, gazing steadfastly, and then, if you took no notice of him, he moved slowly to the next table. If he was given nothing he showed neither disappointment nor anger. If someone offered him a coin he stepped forward a little, stretched out his clawlike hand, took it without a word of thanks and impassively went his way. I had nothing to give him and when he came to me, so that he should not wait in vain, I shook my head.

"Dispense Usted por Dios," I said, using the polite Castilian formula with which the Spaniards refuse a beggar.

But he paid no attention to what I said. He stood in front of me, for as long as he stood at the other tables, looking at me with tragic eyes. I have never seen such a wreck of humanity. There was something terrifying in his appearance. He did not look quite sane. At length he passed on.

It was one o'clock and I had lunch. When I awoke from my siesta it was still very hot, but towards evening a breath of air coming in through the windows which I had at last ventured to open tempted me into the plaza. I sat down under my arcade and ordered a long drink. Presently people in greater numbers filtered into the open space from the surrounding streets, the tables in the restaurants round it filled up, and in the kiosk in the middle the band began to play. The crowd grew thicker. On the free benches people sat huddled together like dark grapes clustered on a stalk. There was a lively hum of conversation. The big black buzzards flew screeching overhead, swooping down when they saw something to pick up, or scurrying away from under the feet of the passers-by. As twilight descended they swarmed, it seemed from all parts of the town, towards the church tower; they circled heavily about it and hoarsely crying, squabbling and jangling, settled themselves uneasily to roost. And again boot-blacks begged me to have my shoes cleaned, news-boys pressed dank papers upon me, beggars whined their plaintive demand for alms. I saw once more that strange, red-bearded fellow and watched him stand motionless, with the crushed and piteous air, before one table after another. He did not stop before mine. I suppose he remembered me from the morning and having failed to get anything from me then thought it useless to try again. You do not often see a red-haired Mexican, and because it was only in Russia that I had seen men of so destitute a mien I asked myself if he was by chance a Russian. It accorded well enough with the Russian fecklessness that he should have allowed himself to sink to such a depth of degradation. Yet he had not a Russian face; his emaciated features were clear-cut, and his blue eyes were not set in the head in a Russian manner; I wondered if he could be a sailor, English, Scandinavian or American, who had deserted his ship and by degrees sunk to this pitiful condition. He disappeared. Since there was nothing else to do, I stayed on till I got hungry, and when I had eaten came back. I sat on till the thinning crowd suggested it was bedtime. I confess that the day had seemed long and I wondered how many similar days I should be forced to spend there.

But I woke after a little while and could not get to sleep again. My room was stifling. I opened the shutters and looked out at the church. There was no moon, but the bright stars faintly lit its outline. The buzzards were closely packed on the cross above the cupola and on the edges of the tower, and now and then they moved a little. The effect was uncanny. And then, I have no notion why, that red scarecrow recurred to my mind and I had suddenly a strange feeling that I had seen him before. It was so vivid that it drove away from me the possibility of sleep. I felt sure that I had come across him, but when and where I could not tell. I tried to picture the surroundings in which he might take his place, but I could see no more than a dim figure against a background of fog. As the dawn approached it grew a little cooler and I was able to sleep.

I spent my second day at Vera Cruz as I had spent the first. But I watched for the coming of the red-haired beggar and as he stood at the tables near mine I examined him with attention. I felt certain now that I had seen him somewhere. I even felt certain that I had known him and talked to him, but I still could recall none of the circumstances. Once more he passed my table without stopping and when his eyes met mine I looked in them for some gleam of recollection. Nothing. I wondered if I had made a mistake and thought I had seen him in the same way as sometimes, by some queer motion of the brain, in the act of doing something you are convinced that you are repeating an action that you have done at some past time. I could not get out of my head the impression that at some moment he had entered into my life. I racked my brains. I was sure now that he was either English or American. But I was shy of addressing him. I went over in my mind the possible occasions when I might have met him. Not to be able to place him exasperated me as it does when you try to remember a name that is on the tip of your tongue and yet eludes you. The day wore on.

Another day came, another morning, another evening. It was Sunday and the plaza was more crowded than ever. The tables under the arcade were packed. As usual the red-haired beggar came along, a terrifying figure in his silence, his threadbare rags and his pitiful distress. He was standing in front of a table only two from mine, mutely beseeching, but without a gesture. Then I saw the policeman who at intervals tried to protect the public from the importunities of all these beggars sneak round a column and give him a resounding whack with his thong. His thin body winced, but he made no protest and showed no resentment; he seemed to accept the stinging blow as in the ordinary course of things and with his slow movements slunk away into the gathering night of the plaza. But the cruel stripe had whipped my memory and suddenly I remembered.

Not his name, that escaped me still, but everything else. He must have recognized me, for I have not changed very much in twenty years, and that was why after that first morning he had never paused in front of my table. Yes, it was twenty years since I had known him. I was spending a winter in Rome and every evening I used to dine in a restaurant in the Via Sistina where you got excellent macaroni and a good bottle of wine. It was frequented by a little band of English and American art students and one or two writers; and we used to stay late into the night engaged in interminable arguments upon art and literature. He used to come in with a young painter who was a friend of his. He was only a boy then, he could not have been more than twenty-two; and with his blue eyes, straight nose and red hair he was pleasing to look at. I remembered that he spoke a great deal of Central America, he had had a job with the American Fruit Company, but had thrown it over because he wanted to be a writer. He was not popular among us because he was arrogant and we were none of us old enough to take the arrogance of youth with tolerance. He thought us poor fish and did not hesitate to tell us so. He would not show us his work, because our praise meant nothing to him and he despised our censure. His vanity was enormous. It irritated us; but some of us were uneasily aware that it might perhaps be justified. Was it possible that the intense consciousness of genius that he had rested on no grounds? He had sacrificed everything to be a writer. He was so certain of himself that he infected some of his friends with his own assurance.

I recalled his high spirits, his vitality, his confidence in the future and his disinterestedness. It was impossible that it was the same man, and yet I was sure of it. I stood up, paid for my drink and went out into the plaza to find him. My thoughts were in a turmoil. I was aghast. I had thought of him now and then and idly wondered what had become of him. I could never have imagined that he was reduced to this frightful misery. There are hundreds, thousands of youths who enter upon the hard calling of the arts with extravagant hopes; but for the most part they come to terms with their mediocrity and find somewhere in life a niche where they can escape starvation. This was awful. I asked myself what had happened. What hopes deferred had broken his spirit, what disappointments shattered him and what lost illusions ground him to the dust? I asked myself if nothing could be done. I walked round the plaza. He was not in the arcades. There was no hope of finding him in the crowd that circled round the bandstand. The light was waning and I was afraid I had lost him. Then I passed the church and saw him sitting on the steps. I cannot describe what a lamentable object he looked. Life had taken him, rent him on its racks, torn him limb from limb, and then flung him, a bleeding wreck, on the stone steps of that church. I went up to him.

"Do you remember Rome?" I said.

He did not move. He did not answer. He took no more notice of me than if I were not standing before him. He did not look at me. His vacant blue eyes rested on the buzzards that were screaming and tearing at some object at the bottom of the steps. I did not know what to do. I took a yellow-backed note out of my pocket and pressed it in his hand. He did not give it a glance. But his hand moved a little, the thin claw-like fingers closed on the note and scrunched it up; he made it into a little ball and then edging it onto his thumb flicked it into the air so that it fell among the jangling buzzards. I turned my head instinctively and saw one of them seize it in his beak and fly off followed by two others screaming behind it. When I looked back the man was gone.

I stayed three more days in Vera Cruz. I never saw him again.

# STRAIGHT FLUSH

I AM NOT A BAD SAILOR and when under stress of weather the game broke up I did not go below. We were in the habit of playing poker into the small hours, a mild game that could hurt nobody, but it had been blowing all day and with nightfall the wind strengthened to half a gale. One or two of our bunch admitted that they felt none too comfortable and one or two others played with unwonted detachment. But even if you are not sick dirty weather at sea is an unpleasant thing. I hate the fool who tells you he loves a storm and tramping the deck lustily vows that it can never be too rough for him. When the woodwork groans and creaks, glasses crash to the floor and you lurch in your chair as the ship heels over, when the wind howls and the waves thunder against the side, I very much prefer dry land. I think no one was sorry when one of the players said he had had enough, and the last round of Jack Pots was agreed to without demur. I remained alone in the smoking-room, for I knew I should not easily get to sleep in that racket and I could not read in bed with any comfort when the North Pacific kept dashing itself against my portholes. I shuffled together the two packs we had been playing with and set out a complicated patience.

I had been playing about ten minutes when the door was opened with a blast of wind that sent my cards flying, and two passengers, rather breathless, slipped into the smoking-room. We were not a full ship and we were ten days out from Hong-Kong so that I had had time to become acquainted with pretty well everyone on board. I had spoken on several occasions to the pair who now entered, and seeing me by myself they came over to my table.

They were very old men, both of them. That perhaps was what had brought them together, for they had first met when they got on board at Hong-Kong, and now you saw them sitting together in the smoking-room most of the day, not talking very much, but just comfortable to be side by side, with a bottle of Vichy water between them. They were very rich old men too and that was a bond between them. The rich feel at ease in one another's company. They know that money means merit. Their experience of the poor is that they always want something. It is true that the poor admire the rich and it is pleasant to be admired, but they envy them as well and this prevents their admiration from being quite candid. Mr Rosenbaum was a little hunched-up Jew, very frail in clothes that looked too big for him.

and he gave you the impression of hanging on to mortality only by a hair. His ancient, emaciated body looked as though it were already attacked by the corruption of the grave. The only expression his face ever bore was one of cunning, but it was purely habitual, the result of ever so many years' astuteness; he was a kindly, friendly person, very free with his drinks and cigars, and his charity was world famous. The other was called Donaldson. He was a Scot, but had gone to California as a little boy and made a great deal of money mining. He was short and stout, with a red, clean-shaven, shiny face and no hair but a sickle of silver above his neck, and very gentle eyes. Whatever force he had had to make his way in the world had been worn away by the years and he was now a picture of mild beneficence.

"I thought you'd turned in long ago," I remarked.

"I should have," returned the Scot, "only Mr Rosenbaum kept me up talking of old times."

"What's the good of going to bed when you can't sleep?" said Mr Rosenbaum.

"Walk ten times round the deck with me tomorrow morning and you'll sleep all right."

"I've never taken any exercise in my life and I'm not going to begin now."

"That's foolishness. You'd be twice the man you are now if you'd taken exercise. Look at me. You'd never think I was seventy-nine, would you?"

Mr Rosenbaum looked critically at Mr Donaldson.

"No, I wouldn't. You're very well preserved. You look younger than me and I'm only seventy-six. But then I never had a chance to take care of myself."

At that moment the steward came up.

"The bar's just going to close, gentlemen. Is there anything I can get you?"

"It's a stormy night," said Mr Rosenbaum. "Let's have a bottle of champagne."

"Small Vichy for me," said Mr Donaldson.

"Oh, very well, small Vichy for me too."

The steward went away.

"But mind you," continued Mr Rosenbaum testily, "I wouldn't have done without the things you've done without, not for all the money in the world."

Mr Donaldson gave me his gentle smile.

"Mr Rosenbaum can't get over it because I've never touched a card nor a drop of alcohol for fifty-seven years."

"Now I ask you, what sort of a life is that?"

"I was a very heavy drinker when I was a young fellow and a desperate gambler, but I had a very terrible experience. It was a lesson to me and I took it."

"Tell him about it," said Mr Rosenbaum. "He's

an author. He'll write it up and perhaps he'll be able to make his passage money."

"It's not a story I like telling very much even now. I'll make it as short as I can. Me and three others had staked out a claim, friends all of us, and the oldest wasn't twenty-five; there was me and my partner and a couple of brothers, McDermott their name was, but they were more like friends than brothers. What was one's was the other's, and one wouldn't go into town without the other went too, and they were always laughing and joking together. A fine clean pair of boys, over six feet high both of them, and handsome. We were a wild bunch and we had pretty good luck on the whole and when we made money we didn't hesitate to spend it. Well, one night we'd all been drinking very heavily and we started a poker game. I guess we were a good deal drunker than we realized. Anyhow suddenly a row started between the McDermotts. One of them accused the other of cheating. 'You take that back,' cried Jamie. 'I'll see you in hell first,' says Eddie. And before me and my partner could do anything Jamie had pulled out his gun and shot his brother dead."

The ship gave a huge roll and we all clung to our seats. In the steward's pantry there was a great clatter as bottles and glasses slid along a shelf. It was strange to hear that grim little story told by that mild old man. It was a story of another age and you could hardly believe that this fat, red-faced little fellow, with his silver fringe of hair, in a dinner jacket, two large pearls in his shirt front, had really taken part in it.

"What happened then?" I asked.

"We sobered up pretty quick. At first Jamie couldn't believe Eddie was dead. He took him in his arms and kept calling him. 'Eddie,' he says, 'wake up, old boy, wake up.' He cried all night and next day we rode in with him to town, forty miles it was, me on one side of him and my partner on the other, and handed him over to the sheriff. I was crying too when we shook hands with him and said good-bye. I told my partner I'd never touch a card again or drink as long as I lived, and I never have, and I never will."

Mr Donaldson looked down, and his lips were trembling. He seemed to see again that scene of long ago. There was one thing I should have liked to ask him about, but he was evidently so much moved I did not like to. They seem not to have hesitated, his partner and himself, but delivered up this wretched boy to justice as though it were the most natural thing in the world. It suggested that even in those rough, wild men the respect for the law had somehow the force of an instinct. A little shiver ran through me. Mr Donaldson emptied his glass of Vichy and with a curt good-night left us.

"The old fellow's getting a bit childish," said Mr Rosenbaum. "I don't believe he was ever very bright."

"Well, apparently he was bright enough to make an awful lot of money."

"But how? In those days in California you didn't want brains to make money, you only wanted luck. I know what I'm talking about. Johannesburg was the place where you had to have your wits about you. Joburg in the eighties. It was grand. We were a tough lot of guys, I can tell you. It was each for himself and the devil take the hindmost."

He took a meditative sip of his Vichy.

"You talk of your cricket and baseball, your golf and tennis and football, you can have them, they're all very well for boys; is it a reasonable thing, I ask you, for a grown man to run about and hit a ball? Poker's the only game fit for a grown man. Then your hand is against every man and every man's hand is against yours. Teamwork? Who ever made a fortune by teamwork? There's only one way to make a fortune and that's to down the fellow who's up against you."

"I didn't know you were a poker player," I interrupted. "Why don't you take a hand one evening?"

"I don't play any more. I've given it up too, but for the only reason a man should. I can't see myself giving it up because a friend of mine was unlucky enough to get killed. Anyway a man who's damn fool enough to get killed isn't worth having as a friend. But in the old days! If you wanted to know what poker was you ought to have been in South Africa then. It was the biggest game I've ever seen. And they were fine players; there wasn't a crooked dodge they weren't up to. It was grand. Just to give you an example, one night I was playing with some of the biggest men in Johannesburg and I was called away. There was a couple of thousand pounds in the pot! 'Deal me a hand, I won't keep you waiting,' I said. 'All right,' they said, 'don't hurry.' Well, I wasn't gone more than a minute. When I came back I picked up my cards and saw I'd got a straight flush to the queen. I didn't say a word, I just threw in my hand. I knew my company. And do you know, I was wrong."

"What do you mean? I don't understand."

"It was a perfectly straight deal and the pot was won on three sevens. But how could I tell that? Naturally I thought someone else had a straight flush to the king. It looked to me just the sort of hand I might lose a hundred thousand pounds on."

"Too bad," I said.

"I very nearly had a stroke. And it was on account of another pat straight flush that I gave up playing poker. I've only had about five in my life."

"I believe the chances are nearly sixty-six thousand to one against."

"In San Francisco it was, the year before last. I'd been playing in poor luck all the evening. I hadn't lost much money because I never had a chance to play. I'd hardly had a pair and if I got a pair I couldn't improve. Then I got a hand just as bad as the others and I didn't come in. The man next me wasn't playing either and I showed him my hand. 'That's the kind of thing I've been getting all the evening,' I said. 'How can anyone be expected to play with cards like that?' 'Well, I don't know what more you want,' he said as he looked at them. 'Most of us would be prepared to come in on a straight flush.' 'What's that?' I cried. I was trembling like a leaf. I looked at the cards again. I thought I had two or three little hearts and two or three little diamonds. It was a straight flush in hearts all right and I hadn't seen it. My eyes, it was. I knew what it meant. Old age. I don't cry much. I'm not that sort of man. But I couldn't help it then. I tried to control myself, but the tears just rolled down my cheeks. Then I got up. 'I'm through, gentlemen,' I said. 'When a man's eyes are so dim that he can't see a straight flush when it's dealt him he has no business to play poker. Nature's given me a hint and I'm taking it. I'll never play poker again as long as I live.' I cashed in my chips, all but one, and I left the house. I've never played since."

Mr Rosenbaum took a chip out of his waistcoat pocket and showed it to me.

"I kept this as a souvenir. I always carry it about with me. I'm a sentimental old fool, I know that, but you see, poker was the only thing I cared for. Now I've only got one thing left."

"What is that?" I asked.

A smile flickered across his cunning little face and behind his thick glasses his rheumy eyes twinkled with ironic glee. He looked incredibly astute and malicious. He gave the thin, high-pitched cackle of an old man amused and answered with a single word:

"Philanthropy."

# THE VERGER

THERE HAD BEEN a christening that afternoon at St Peter's, Neville Square, and Albert Edward Foreman still wore his verger's gown. He kept his new one, its folds as full and stiff as though it were made not of alpaca but of perennial bronze, for funerals and weddings (St Peter's, Neville Square, was a church much favoured by the fashionable for these ceremonies) and now he wore only his second best. He wore it with complacence, for it was the dignified symbol of his office, and without it (when he took it off to go home) he had the disconcerting sensation of being somewhat insufficiently clad. He took pains with it; he pressed it and ironed it himself. During the sixteen years he had been verger of this church he had had a succession of such gowns, but he had never been able to throw them away when they were worn out and the complete series, neatly wrapped up in brown paper, lay in the bottom drawer of the wardrobe in his bedroom.

The verger busied himself quietly, replacing the painted wooden cover on the marble font, taking away a chair that had been brought for an infirm old lady, and waited for the vicar to have finished in the vestry so that he could tidy up in there and go home. Presently he saw him walk across the chancel, genuflect in front of the high altar and come down the aisle; but he still wore his cassock.

"What's he 'anging about for?" the verger said to himself. "Don't 'e know I want my tea?"

The vicar had been but recently appointed, a red-faced energetic man in the early forties, and Albert Edward still regretted his predecessor, a clergyman of the old school who preached leisurely sermons in a silvery voice and dined out a great deal with his more aristocratic parishioners. He liked things in church to be just so, but he never fussed; he was not like this new man who wanted to have his finger in every pie. But Albert Edward was tolerant. St Peter's was in a very good neighbourhood and the parishioners were a very nice class of people. The new vicar had come from the East End and he couldn't be expected to fall in all at once with the discreet ways of his fashionable congregation.

"All this 'ustle," said Albert Edward. "But give 'im time, he'll learn."

When the vicar had walked down the aisle so far that he could address the verger without raising his voice more than was becoming in a place of worship he stopped.

"Foreman, will you come into the vestry for a minute. I have something to say to you."

"Very good, sir."

The vicar waited for him to come up and they walked up the church together.

"A very nice christening, I thought, sir. Funny 'ow the baby stopped cryin' the moment you took him."

"I've noticed they very often do," said the vicar, with a little smile. "After all I've had a good deal of practice with them."

It was a source of subdued pride to him that he could nearly always quiet a whimpering infant by the manner in which he held it and he was not unconscious of the amused admiration with which mothers and nurses watched him settle the baby in the crook of his surpliced arm. The verger knew that it pleased him to be complimented on his talent.

The vicar preceded Albert Edward into the vestry. Albert Edward was a trifle surprised to find the two churchwardens there. He had not seen them come in. They gave him pleasant nods.

"Good-afternoon, my lord. Good-afternoon, sir," he said to one ofter the other.

They were elderly men, both of them, and they had been churchwardens almost as long as Albert Edward had been verger. They were sitting now at a handsome refectory table that the old vicar had brought many years before from Italy and the vicar sat down in the vacant chair between them. Albert

Edward faced them, the table between him and them, and wondered with slight uneasiness what was the matter. He remembered still the occasion on which the organist had got into trouble and the bother they had all had to hush things up. In a church like St Peter's, Neville Square, they couldn't afford a scandal. On the vicar's red face was a look of resolute benignity, but the others bore an expression that was slightly troubled.

"He's been naggin' them, he 'as," said the verger to himself. "He's jockeyed them into doin' something, but they don't 'alf like it. That's what it is, you mark my words."

But his thoughts did not appear on Albert Edward's clean-cut and distinguished features. He stood in a respectful but not obsequious attitude. He had been in service before he was appointed to his ecclesiastical office, but only in very good houses, and his deportment was irreproachable. Starting as a page-boy in the household of a merchant-prince he had risen by due degrees from the position of fourth to first footman, for a year he had been single-handed butler to a widowed peeress and, till the vacancy occurred at St Peter's, butler with two men under him in the house of a retired ambassador. He was tall, spare, grave and dignified. He looked, if not like a duke, at least like an actor of the old school who specialized in dukes' parts. He had tact, firmness and self-assurance. His character was unimpeachable.

The vicar began briskly.

"Foreman, we've got something rather unpleasant to say to you. You've been here a great many years and I think his lordship and the general agree with me that you've fulfilled the duties of your office to the satisfaction of everybody concerned."

The two churchwardens nodded.

"But a most extraordinary circumstance came to my knowledge the other day and I felt it my duty to impart it to the churchwardens. I discovered to my astonishment that you could neither read nor write."

The verger's face betrayed no sign of embarrassment.

"The last vicar knew that, sir," he replied. "He said it didn't make no difference. He always said there was a great deal too much education in the world for 'is taste."

"It's the most amazing thing I ever heard," cried the general. "Do you mean to say that you've been verger of this church for sixteen years and never learned to read or write?"

"I went into service when I was twelve, sir. The cook in the first place tried to teach me once, but I didn't seem to 'ave the knack for it, and then what with one thing and another I never seemed to 'ave the time. I've never really found the want of it. I think a lot of these young fellows waste a rare lot of time readin' when they might be doin' something useful."

"But don't you want to know the news?" said the other churchwarden. "Don't you ever want to write a letter?"

"No, me lord, I seem to manage very well without. And of late years now they've all these pictures in the papers I get to know what's goin' on pretty well. Me wife's quite a scholar and if I want to write a letter she writes it for me. It's not as if I was a bettin' man."

The two churchwardens gave the vicar a troubled glance and then looked down at the table.

"Well, Foreman, I've talked the matter over with these gentlemen and they quite agree with me that the situation is impossible. At a church like St Peter's, Neville Square, we cannot have a verger who can neither read nor write."

Albert Edward's thin, sallow face reddened and he moved uneasily on his feet, but he made no reply.

"Understand me, Foreman, I have no complaint to make against you. You do your work quite satisfactorily; I have the highest opinion both of your character and of your capacity; but we haven't the right to take the risk of some accident that might happen owing to your lamentable ignorance. It's a matter of prudence as well as of principle."

"But couldn't you learn, Foreman?" asked the general.

"No, sir, I'm afraid I couldn't, not now. You see I'm not as young as I was and if I couldn't seem able to get the letters in me 'ead when I was a nipper I don't think there's much chance of it now."

"We don't want to be harsh with you, Foreman," said the vicar. "But the churchwardens and I have quite made up our minds. We'll give you three months and if at the end of that time you cannot read and write I'm afraid you'll have to go."

Albert Edward had never liked the new vicar. He'd said from the beginning that they'd made a mistake when they gave him St Peter's. He wasn't the type of man they wanted with a classy congregation like that. And now he straightened himself a little. He knew his value and he wasn't going to allow himself to be put upon.

"I'm very sorry, sir, I'm afraid it's no good. I'm too old a dog to learn new tricks. I've lived a good many years without knowin' 'ow to read and write and without wishin' to praise myself, self-praise is no recommendation, I don't mind sayin' I've done my duty in that state of life in which it 'as pleased a merciful providence to place me, and if I *could* learn now I don't know as I'd want to."

"In that case, Foreman, I'm afraid you must go."

"Yes, sir, I quite understand. I shall be 'appy to 'and in my resignation as soon as you've found somebody to take my place."

But when Albert Edward with his usual politeness had closed the church door behind the vicar and the two churchwardens he could not sustain the air of unruffled dignity with which he had borne the blow inflicted upon him and his lips quivered. He walked slowly back to the vestry and hung up on its proper peg his verger's gown. He sighed as he thought of all the grand funerals and smart weddings it had seen. He tidied everything up, put on his coat, and hat in hand walked down the aisle. He locked the church door behind him. He strolled across the square, but deep in his sad thoughts he did not take the street that led him home, where a nice strong cup of tea awaited him; he took the wrong turning. He walked slowly along. His heart was heavy. He did not know what he should do with himself. He did not fancy the notion of going back to domestic service; after being his own master for so many years, for the vicar and churchwardens could say what they liked, it was he that had run

St Peter's, Neville Square, he could scarcely demean himself by accepting a situation. He had saved a tidy sum, but not enough to live on without doing something, and life seemed to cost more every year. He had never thought to be troubled with such questions. The vergers of St Peter's, like the popes of Rome, were there for life. He had often thought of the pleasant reference the vicar would make in his sermon at evensong the first Sunday after his death to the long and faithful service and the exemplary character of their late verger Albert Edward Foreman. He sighed deeply. Albert Edward was a non-smoker and a total abstainer, but with a certain latitude; that is to say he liked a glass of beer with his dinner and when he was tired he enjoyed a cigarette. It occurred to him now that one would comfort him and since he did not carry them he looked about him for a shop where he could buy a packet of Gold Flakes. He did not at once see one and walked on a little. It was a long street, with all sorts of shops in it, but there was not a single one where you could buy cigarettes.

"That's strange," said Albert Edward.

To make sure he walked right up the street again. No, there was no doubt about it. He stopped and looked reflectively up and down.

"I can't be the only man as walks along this street

and wants a fag," he said. "I shouldn't wonder but what a fellow might do very well with a little shop here. Tobacco and sweets, you know."

He gave a sudden start.

"That's an idea," he said. "Strange 'ow things come to you when you least expect it."

He turned, walked home, and had his tea.

"You're very silent this afternoon, Albert," his wife remarked.

"I'm thinkin'," he said.

He considered the matter from every point of view and next day he went along the street and by good luck found a little shop to let that looked as though it would exactly suit him. Twenty-four hours later he had taken it and when a month after that he left St Peter's, Neville Square, for ever, Albert Edward Foreman set up in business as a tobacconist and newsagent. His wife said it was a dreadful come-down after being verger of St Peter's, but he answered that you had to move with the times, the church wasn't what it was, and 'enceforward he was going to render unto Caesar what was Caesar's. Albert Edward did very well. He did so well that in a year or so it struck him that he might take a second shop and put a manager in. He looked for another long street that hadn't got a tobacconist in it and when he found it, and a shop to let, took it and stocked it. This was a success too. Then it occurred to him that if he could run two he could run half a dozen, so he began walking about London, and whenever he found a long street that had no tobacconist and a shop to let he took it. In the course of ten years he had acquired no less than ten shops and he was making money hand over fist. He went round to all of them himself every Monday, collected the week's takings and took them to the bank.

One morning when he was there paying in a bundle of notes and a heavy bag of silver the cashier told him that the manager would like to see him. He was shown into an office and the manager shook hands with him.

"Mr Foreman, I wanted to have a talk to you about the money you've got on deposit with us. D'you know exactly how much it is?"

"Not within a pound or two, sir; but I've got a pretty rough idea."

"Apart from what you paid in this morning it's a little over thirty thousand pounds. That's a very large sum to have on deposit and I should have thought you'd do better to invest it."

"I wouldn't want to take no risk, sir. I know it's safe in the bank."

"You needn't have the least anxiety. We'll make

you out a list of absolutely gilt-edged securities. They'll bring you in a better rate of interest than we can possibly afford to give you."

A troubled look settled on Mr Foreman's distinguished face.

"I've never 'ad anything to do with stocks and shares and I'd 'ave to leave it all in your 'ands," he said.

The manager smiled.

"We'll do everything. All you'll have to do next time you come in is just to sign the transfers."

"I could do that all right," said Albert uncertainly. "But 'ow should I know what I was signin'?"

"I suppose you can read," said the manager a trifle sharply.

Mr Foreman gave him a disarming smile.

"Well, sir, that's just it. I can't. I know it sounds funny like, but there it is, I can't read or write, only me name, an' I only learnt to do that when I went into business."

The manager was so surprised that he jumped up from his chair.

"That's the most extraordinary thing I ever heard."

"You see, it's like this, sir, I never 'ad the opportunity until it was too late and then some'ow I wouldn't. I got obstinate like."

The manager stared at him as though he were a prehistoric monster.

"And do you mean to say that you've built up this important business and amassed a fortune of thirty thousand pounds without being able to read or write? Good God, man, what would you be now if you had been able to?"

"I can tell you that, sir," said Mr Foreman, a little smile on his still aristocratic features. "I'd be verger of St Peter's, Neville Square."

# THE WASH TUB

Positano stands on the side of a steep hill, a disarray of huddled white houses, their tiled roofs washed pale by the suns of a hundred years; but unlike many of these Italian towns perched out of harm's way on a rocky eminence it does not offer you at one delightful glance all it has to give. It has quaint streets that zigzag up the hill and battered, painted houses in the baroque style, but very late, in which Neapolitan noblemen led for a season lives of penurious grandeur. It is indeed almost excessively picturesque and in winter its two or three modest hotels are crowded with painters, male and female, who in their different ways acknowledge by their daily labours the emotion it has excited in them. Some take infinite pains to place on canvas every window and every tile their peering eyes can discover and doubtless achieve the satisfaction that rewards honest industry. "At all events it's sincere," they say modestly when they show you their work. Some, rugged and dashing, in a fine frenzy attack their canvas with a pallet knife charged with a wad of paint, and they say: "You see, what I was trying to bring out was my personality." They slightly close their eyes and tentatively murmur: "I think it's rather me, don't you?" And there are some who give you highly entertaining arrangements of spheres and cubes and mutter sombrely: "That's how I see it!" These for the most part are strong silent men who waste no words.

But Positano looks full south and the chances are that in summer you will have it to yourself. The hotel is clean and cool and there is a terrace, overhung with vines, where you can sit at night and look at the sea bespangled with dim stars. Down at the Marina, on the quay, is a little tavern where you can dine under an archway off anchovies and ham, macaroni and fresh-caught mullet, and drink cold wine. Once a day the steamer from Naples comes in, bringing the mail, and for a quarter of an hour gives the beach (there is no port and the passengers are landed in small boats) an air of animation.

One August, tiring of Capri where I had been staying, I made up my mind to spend a few days at Positano, so I hired a fishing-boat and rowed over. I stopped on the way in a shady cove to bathe and lunch and sleep, and did not arrive till evening. I strolled up the hill, my two bags following me on the heads of two sturdy women, to the hotel, and was surprised to learn that I was not its only guest. The waiter, whose name was Giuseppe, was an old friend of mine, and at that season he was boots, porter, chambermaid and cook as well. He told me that an American signore had been staying there for three months.

"Is he a painter or a writer or something?" I asked.

"No, signore, he's a gentleman."

Odd, I thought. No foreigners came to Positano at that time of year but German Wandervögel, looking hot and dusty, with satchels on their backs; and they only stayed overnight. I could not imagine anyone wishing to spend three months there; unless of course he were hiding. And since all London had been excited by the flight earlier in the year of an eminent, but dishonest, financier, the amusing thought occurred to me that this mysterious stranger was perhaps he. I knew him slightly and trusted that my sudden arrival would not disconcert him.

"You'll see the Signore at the Marina," said Giuseppe, as I was setting out to go down again. "He always dines there."

He was certainly not there when I arrived. I asked what there was for dinner and drank an americano, which is by no means a bad substitute for a cocktail. In a few minutes, however, a man walked in who could be no other than my fellow-guest at the hotel and I had a moment's disappointment when I saw that he was not the absconding financier. A tall, elderly man, bronzed after his summer on the Mediterranean, with a handsome, thin face. He wore a very neat, even smart, suit of cream-coloured silk and no hat. His gray hair was cut very short, but was still thick. There was ease in his bearing, and elegance. He looked round the half-dozen tables under the archway at which the natives of the place were playing cards or dominoes and his eyes rested on me. They smiled pleasantly. He came up.

"I hear you have just arrived at the hotel. Giuseppe suggested that as he couldn't come down here to effect an introduction you wouldn't mind if I introduced myself. Would it bore you to dine with a total stranger?"

"Of course not. Sit down."

He turned to the maid who was laying a cover for me and in beautiful Italian told her that I would eat with him. He looked at my americano.

"I have got them to stock a little gin and French vermouth for me. Would you allow me to mix you a very dry martini?"

"Without hesitation."

"It gives an exotic note to the surroundings which brings out the local colour."

He certainly made a very good cocktail and with

added appetite we ate the ham and anchovies with which our dinner began. My host had a pleasant humour and his fluent conversation was agreeable.

"You must forgive me if I talk too much," he said presently. "This is the first chance I've had to speak English for three months. I don't suppose you will stay here long and I mean to make the most of it."

"Three months is a long time to stay at Positano."

"I've hired a boat and I bathe and fish. I read a great deal. I have a good many books here and if there's anything I can lend you I shall be very glad."

"I think I have enough reading matter. But I should love to look at what you have. It's always fun looking at other people's books."

He gave me a sharp look and his eyes twinkled.

"It also tells you a good deal about them," he murmured.

When we finished dinner we went on talking. The stranger was well read and interested in a diversity of topics. He spoke with so much knowledge of painting that I wondered if he was an art critic or a dealer. But then it appeared that he had been reading Suetonius and I came to the conclusion that he was a college professor. I asked him his name.

"Barnaby," he answered.

"That's a name that has recently acquired an amazing celebrity."

"Oh, how so?"

"Have you never heard of the celebrated Mrs Barnaby? She's a compatriot of yours."

"I admit that I've seen her name in the papers rather frequently of late. Do you know her?"

"Yes, quite well. She gave the grandest parties all last season and I went to them whenever she asked me. Everyone did. She's an astounding woman. She came to London to do the season, and, by George, she did it. She just swept everything before her."

"I understand she's very rich?"

"Fabulously, I believe, but it's not that that has made her success. Plenty of American women have money. Mrs Barnaby has got where she has by sheer force of character. She never pretends to be anything but what she is. She's natural. She's priceless. You know her history, of course?"

My friend smiled.

"Mrs Barnaby may be a great celebrity in London, but to the best of my belief in America she is almost inconceivably unknown."

I smiled also, but within me; I could well imagine how shocked this distinguished and cultured man would be by the rollicking humour, the frankness, with its tang of the soil, and the rich and vital experience of the amazing Mrs Barnaby.

"Well, I'll tell you about her. Her husband appears to be a very rough diamond; he's a great hulking fellow, she says, who could fell a steer with his fist. He's known in Arizona as One-bullet Mike."

"Good gracious. Why?"

"Well, years ago in the old days he killed two men with a single shot. She says he's handier with his gun even now than any man West of the Rockies. He's a miner, but he's been a cowpuncher, a gun-runner and God knows what in his day."

"A thoroughly Western type," said my professor, a trifle acidly I thought.

"Something of a desperado, I imagine. Mrs Barnaby's stories about him are a real treat. Of course everyone's been begging her to let him come over, but she says he'd never leave the wide-open spaces. He struck oil a year or two ago and now he's got all the money in the world. He must be a great character. I've heard her keep the whole dinner-table spellbound when she's talked of the old days when they roughed it together. It gives you quite a thrill when you see this gray-haired woman, not at all pretty, but exquisitely dressed, with the most wonderful pearls, and hear her tell how she washed the miners' clothes and cooked for the camp. Your American women have an adaptability that's really stupendous. When you see Mrs Barnaby sitting at the head of her table, perfectly at home with princes of the blood, ambassadors, cabinet ministers and the duke of this and the duke of that, it seems almost incredible that only a few years ago she was cooking the food of seventy miners."

"Can she read or write?"

"I suppose her invitations are written by her secretary, but she's by no means an ignorant woman. She told me she used to make a point of reading for an hour every night after the fellows in camp had gone to bed."

"Remarkable!"

"On the other hand One-bullet Mike only learnt to write his name when he suddenly found himself under the necessity of signing cheques."

We walked up the hill to our hotel and before separating for the night arranged to take our luncheon with us next day and row over to a cove that my friend had discovered. We spent a charming day bathing, reading, eating, sleeping and talking, and we dined together in the evening. The following morning, after breakfast on the terrace, I reminded Barnaby of his promise to show me his books.

"Come right along."

I accompanied him to his bedroom where Giuseppe, the waiter, was making his bed. The first thing I caught sight of was a photograph in a gorgeous frame of the celebrated Mrs Barnaby. My friend caught sight of it too and suddenly turned pale with anger.

"You fool, Giuseppe. Why have you taken that photograph out of my wardrobe? Why the devil did you think I put it away?"

"I didn't know, signore. That's why I put it back on the signore's table. I thought he liked to see the portrait of his signora."

I was staggered.

"Is my Mrs Barnaby your wife?" I cried.

"She is."

"Good lord, are you One-bullet Mike?"

"Do I look it?"

I began to laugh.

"I'm bound to say you don't."

I glanced at his hands. He smiled grimly and held them out.

"No, sir, I have never felled a steer with my naked fist."

For a moment we stared at one another in silence.

"She'll never forgive me," he moaned. "She wanted me to take a false name, and when I wouldn't she was quite vexed with me. She said it wasn't safe. I said it was bad enough to hide myself in Positano for three months, but I'd be damned if I'd use any other name than my own." He hesitated. "I throw myself on your mercy. I can do nothing but trust to your generosity not to disclose a secret that you have discovered by the most unlikely chance."

"I will be as silent as the grave, but honestly I don't understand. What does it all mean?"

"I am a doctor by profession and for the last thirty years my wife and I have lived in Pennsylvania. I don't know if I have struck you as a roughneck, but I venture to say that Mrs Barnaby is one of the most cultivated women I have ever known. Then a cousin of hers died and left her a very large fortune. There's no mistake about that. My wife is a very, very rich woman. She has always read a great deal of English fiction and her one desire was to have a London season and entertain and do all the grand things she had read about in books. It was her money and although the prospect did not particularly tempt me, I was very glad that she should gratify her wish. We sailed last April. The young Duke and Duchess of Hereford happened to be on board."

"I know. It was they who first launched Mrs Barnaby. They were crazy about her. They've boomed her like an army of press agents."

"I was ill when we sailed, I had a carbuncle which confined me to my stateroom, and Mrs Barnaby was left to look after herself. Her deck chair happened to be next the duchess's and from a remark she overheard it occurred to her that the English aristocracy were not so wrapped up in our social leaders as one might have expected. My wife is a quick little woman and she remarked to me that if you had an ancestor who signed Magna Charta perhaps you were not excessively impressed because the grandfather of one of your acquaintances sold skunks and the grandfather of another ran ferry boats. My wife has a very keen sense of humour. Getting into conversation with the duchess she told her a little Western anecdote and to make it more interesting told it as having happened to herself. Its success was immediate. The duchess begged for another and my wife ventured a little further. Twenty-four hours later she had the duke and duchess eating out of her hand. She used to come down to my stateroom at intervals and tell me of her progress. In the innocence of my heart I was tickled to death and since I had nothing else to do, I sent to the library for the works of Bret Harte and primed her with effective touches."

I slapped my forehead.

"We said she was as good as Bret Harte," I cried.

"I had a grand time thinking of the consternation of my wife's friends when at the end of the voyage I appeared and we told them the truth. But I reckoned without my wife. The day before we reached Southampton Mrs Barnaby told me that the Herefords were arranging parties for her. The duchess was crazy to introduce her to all sorts of wonderful people. It was a chance in a thousand; but of course I would spoil everything; she admitted that she had been forced by the course of events to represent me as very different from what I was. I did not know that she had already transformed me into One-bullet Mike, but I had a shrewd suspicion that she had forgotten to mention that I was on board. Well, to make a long story short, she asked me to go to Paris for a week or two till she had consolidated her position. I didn't mind that. I was much more inclined to do a little work at the Sorbonne than to go to parties in Mayfair, and so, leaving her to go on to Southampton, I got off at Cherbourg. But when I had been in Paris ten days she flew over to see me. She told me that her success had exceeded her wildest dreams: it was ten times more wonderful than any of the novels; but my appearance would ruin it all. Very well, I said, I would stay in Paris. She didn't like the idea of that; she said she'd never have a moment's peace so long as I was so near and might run across someone who knew me. I suggested Vienna or Rome. They wouldn't do either, and at last I came here and here have I been hiding like a criminal for three interminable months."

"Do you mean to say you never killed the two gamblers, shooting one with your right hand and the other with your left?"

"Sir, I have never fired a pistol in my life."

"And what about the attack on your log cabin by the Mexican bandits when your wife loaded your guns for you and you stood the siege for three days till the federal troops rescued you?"

Mr Barnaby smiled grimly.

"I never heard that one. Isn't it a trifle crude?"

"Crude! It was as good as any Wild West picture."

"If I may venture a guess that is where my wife in all probability got the idea."

"But the wash tub. Washing the miners' clothes and all that. You don't know how she made us roar with that story. Why, she swam into London Society in her wash tub."

I began to laugh.

"She's made the most gorgeous fools of us all," I said.

"She's made a pretty considerable fool of me, I

would have you observe," remarked Mr Barnaby.

"She's a marvellous woman and you're right to be proud of her. I always said she was priceless. She realized the passion for romance that beats in every British heart and she's given us exactly what we wanted. I wouldn't betray her for worlds."

"It's all very fine for you, sir. London may have gained a wonderful hostess, but I'm beginning to think that I have lost a perfectly good wife."

"The only place for One-bullet Mike is the great open West. My dear Mr Barnaby, there is only one course open to you now. You must continue to disappear."

"I'm very much obliged to you."

I thought he replied with a good deal of acidity.

# THE SOCIAL SENSE

I DO NOT LIKE long-standing engagements. How can you tell whether on a certain day three or four weeks ahead you will wish to dine with a certain person? The chances are that in the interval something will turn up that you would much sooner do and so long a notice presages a large and formal party. But what help is there? The date has been fixed thus far away so that the guests bidden may be certainly disengaged and it needs a very adequate excuse to prevent your refusal from seeming churlish. You accept, and for a month the engagement hangs over you with gloomy menace. It interferes with your cherished plans. It disorganizes your life. There is really only one way to cope with the situation and that is to put yourself off at the last moment. But it is one that I have never had the courage or the want of scruple to adopt.

It was with a faint sense of resentment then that one June evening towards half-past eight I left my lodging in Half Moon Street to walk round the corner to dine with the Macdonalds. I liked them. Many years ago I made up my mind not to eat the food of persons I disliked or despised, and though

I have on this account enjoyed the hospitality of far fewer people than I otherwise should have done I still think the rule a good one. The Macdonalds were nice, but their parties were a toss-up. They suffered from the delusion that if they asked six persons to dine with them who had nothing in the world to say to one another the party would be a failure, but if they multiplied it by three and asked eighteen it must be a success. I arrived a little late, which is almost inevitable when you live so near the house you are going to that it is not worth while to take a taxi, and the room into which I was shown was filled with people. I knew few of them and my heart sank as I saw myself laboriously making conversation through a long dinner with two total strangers. It was a relief to me when I saw Thomas and Mary Warton come in and an unexpected pleasure when I found on going in to dinner that I had been placed next to Mary.

Thomas Warton was a portrait painter who at one time had had considerable success, but he had never fulfilled the promise of his youth and had long ceased to be taken seriously by the critics. He made an adequate income, but at the Private View of the Royal Academy no one gave more than a passing glance at the dull but conscientious portraits of fox-hunting squires and prosperous merchants which with unfailing regularity he sent to the annual exhibition. One would have liked to admire his work because he was an amiable and kindly man. If you happened to be a writer he was so genuinely enthusiastic over anything you had done, so charmed with any success you might have had, that you wished your conscience would allow you to speak with decent warmth of his own productions. It was impossible and you were driven to the last refuge of the portrait painter's friend.

"It looks as if it were a marvellous likeness," you said.

Mary Warton had been in her day a well-known concert singer and she had still the remains of a lovely voice. She must in her youth have been very handsome. Now, at fifty-three, she had a haggard look. Her features were rather mannish and her skin was weather-beaten; but her short gray hair was thick and curly and her fine eyes were bright with intelligence. She dressed picturesquely rather than fashionably and she had a weakness for strings of beads and fantastic earrings. She had a blunt manner, a quick sense of human folly and a sharp tongue, so that many people did not like her. But no one could deny that she was clever. She was not only an accomplished musician, but she was a great reader and she was passionately interested in painting. She had a very rare feeling for art. She liked the modern, not from pose but from natural inclination, and she had bought for next to nothing the pictures of unknown painters who later became famous. You heard at her house the most recent and difficult music and no poet or novelist in Europe could offer the world something new and strange without her being ready to fight on his behalf the good fight against the Philistines. You might say she was a highbrow: she was; but her taste was almost faultless, her judgement sound and her enthusiasm unaffected.

No one admired her more than Thomas Warton. He had fallen in love with her when she was still a singer and had pestered her to marry him. She had refused him half a dozen times and I had a notion that she had married him in the end with hesitation. She thought that he would become a great painter and when he turned out to be no more than a decent craftsman, without originality or imagination, she felt that she had been cheated. She was mortified by the contempt with which the connoisseurs regarded him. Thomas Warton loved his wife. He had the greatest respect for her judgement and would sooner have had a word of praise from her than columns of eulogy in all the papers in London. She was too honest to say what she did not think. It wounded him bitterly that she held his work in such poor esteem, and though he pretended to make a joke of it you could see that at heart he resented her outspoken comments. Sometimes his long, horselike face grew red with the anger he tried to control and his eyes dark with hatred. It was notorious among their friends that the couple did not get on. They had the distressing habit of fripping in public. Warton never spoke to others of Mary but with admiration, but she was less discreet and her confidants knew how exasperating she found him. She admitted his goodness, his generosity, his unselfishness; she admitted them ungrudgingly; but his defects were of the sort that make a man hard to live with, for he was narrow, argumentative and conceited. He was not an artist and Mary Warton cared more for art than for anything in the world. It was a matter on which she could not compromise. It blinded her to the fact that the faults in Warton that maddened her were due in large part to his hurt feelings. She wounded him continually and he was dogmatic and intolerant in self-protection. There cannot be anything much worse than to be despised by the one person whose approval is all in all to you; and though Thomas Warton was intolerable it was impossible not to feel sorry for him. But if I have given the impression that Mary was a discontented, rather tiresome, pretentious woman I have been unjust to her. She was a loyal friend and a delightful companion. You could talk to her of any subject under the sun. Her conversation was humorous and witty. Her vitality was immense.

She was sitting now on the left hand of her host and the talk around her was general. I was occupied with my next-door neighbour, but I guessed by the laughter with which Mary's sallies were greeted that she was at her brilliant best. When she was in the vein no one could approach her.

"You're in great form tonight," I remarked, when at last she turned to me.

"Does it surprise you?"

"No, it's what I expect of you. No wonder people tumble over one another to get you to their houses. You have the inestimable gift of making a party go."

"I do my little best to earn my dinner."

"By the way, how's Manson? Someone told me the other day that he was going into a nursing home for an operation. I hope it's nothing serious."

Mary paused for a moment before answering, but she still smiled brightly.

"Haven't you seen the paper tonight?"

"No, I've been playing golf. I only got home in time to jump into a bath and change."

"He died at two o'clock this afternoon." I was about to make an exclamation of horrified surprise, but she stopped me. "Take care. Tom is watching me like a lynx. They're all watching me. They all know I adored him, but they none of them know for certain if he was my lover, even Tom doesn't know; they want to see how I'm taking it. Try to look as if you were talking of the Russian Ballet."

At that moment someone addressed her from the other side of the table, and throwing back her head a little with a gesture that was habitual with her, a smile on her large mouth, she flung at the speaker so quick and apt an answer that everyone round her burst out laughing. The talk once more became general and I was left to my consternation.

I knew, everyone knew, that for five and twenty years there had existed between Gerrard Manson and Mary Warton a passionate attachment. It had lasted so long that even the more straitlaced of their friends, if ever they had been shocked by it, had long since learnt to accept it with tolerance. They were middle-aged people, Manson was sixty and Mary not much younger, and it was absurd that at their age they should not do what they liked. You met them sometimes sitting in a retired corner of an obscure restaurant or walking together in the Zoo and you wondered why they still took care to conceal an affair that was nobody's business but their own. But of course there was Thomas. He was insanely jealous of Mary. He made violent scenes and indeed, at the end of one tempestuous period, not so very long ago, he had forced her to promise never to see Manson again. Of course she broke the promise, and though she knew that Thomas suspected this, she took precautions to prevent him from discovering it for a fact.

It was hard on Thomas. I think he and Mary would have jogged on well enough together and she would have resigned herself to the fact that he was a second-rate painter if her intercourse with Manson had not embittered her judgement. The contrast between her husband's mediocrity and her lover's brilliance was too galling.

"With Tom I feel as if I were stifling in a closed room full of dusty knickknacks," she told me. "With Gerrard I breathe the pure air of the mountain tops."

"Is it possible for a woman to fall in love with a man's mind?" I asked in a pure spirit of inquiry.

"What else is there in Gerrard?"

That, I admit, was a poser. For my part I thought, nothing; but the sex is extraordinary and I was quite ready to believe that Mary saw in Gerrard Manson a charm and a physical attractiveness to which most people were blind. He was a shrivelled little man, with a pale intellectual face, faded blue eyes behind his spectacles, and a high dome of shiny bald head. He had none of the appearance of a romantic lover. On the other hand he was certainly a very subtle critic and a felicitous essayist. I resented somewhat his contemptuous attitude towards English writers unless they were safely dead and buried; but this was only to his credit with the intelligentsia, who are ever ready to believe that there can be no good in what is produced in their own country, and with them his influence was great. On one occasion I told him that one had only to put a commonplace in French for him to mistake it for an epigram and he had thought well enough of the joke to use it as his own in one of his essays. He reserved such praise as he was willing to accord his contemporaries to those who wrote in a foreign tongue. The exasperating thing was that no one could deny that he was himself a brilliant writer. His style was exquisite. His knowledge was vast. He could be profound without pomposity, amusing without frivolity, and polished without affectation. His slightest article was readable. His essays were little masterpieces. For my part I did not find him a very agreeable companion. Perhaps I did not get the best out of him. Though I knew him a great many years I never heard him say an amusing thing. He was not talkative and when he made a remark it was oracular. The prospect of spending an evening alone with him would have filled me with dismay. It never ceased to puzzle me that this dull and mannered little man should be able to write with so much grace, wit and gaiety.

It puzzled me even more than that a gallant and vivacious creature like Mary Warton should have cherished for him so consuming a passion. These things are inexplicable and there was evidently something in that odd, crabbed, irascible creature that appealed to women. His wife adored him. She was a fat, frowzy, boring person. She had led Gerrard a dog's life, but had always refused to give him his freedom. She swore to kill herself if he left her and since she was unbalanced and hysterical he was never quite certain that she would not carry out her threat. One day, when I was having tea with Mary, I saw that she was distraught and nervous and when I asked her what was the matter she burst into tears. She had been lunching with Manson and had found him shattered after a terrific scene with his wife.

"We can't go on like this," Mary cried. "It's ruining his life. It's ruining all our lives."

"Why don't you take the plunge?"

"What do you mean?"

"You've been lovers so long, you know the best and the worst of one another by now; you're getting old and you can't count on many more years of life; it seems a pity to waste a love that has endured so long. What good are you doing to Mrs Manson or to Tom? Are they happy because you two are making yourselves miserable?"

"No."

"Then why don't you chuck everything and just go off together and let come what may?"

Mary shook her head.

"We've talked that over endlessly. We've talked it over for a quarter of a century. It's impossible. For years Gerrard couldn't on account of his daughters. Mrs Manson may have been a very fond mother, but she was a very bad one, and there was no one to see the girls were properly brought up but Gerrard. And now that they're married off he's set in his habits. What should we do? Go to France or Italy? I couldn't tear Gerrard away from his surroundings. He'd be wretched. He's too old to make a fresh start. And besides, though Thomas nags me and makes scenes and we frip and get on one another's nerves, he loves me. When it came to the point I simply shouldn't have the heart to leave him. He'd be lost without me."

"It's a situation without an issue. I'm dreadfully sorry for you."

On a sudden Mary's haggard, weather-beaten face was lit by a smile that broke on her large red mouth; and upon my word at that moment she was beautiful.

"You need not be. I was rather low a little while ago, but now I've had a good cry I feel better. Notwithstanding all the pain, all the unhappiness this affair has caused me, I wouldn't have missed it for all the world. For those few moments of ecstasy my love has brought me I would be willing to live all my life over again. And I think he'd tell you the same thing. Oh, it's been so infinitely worth while."

I could not help but be moved.

"There's no doubt about it," I said. "That's love all right."

"Yes, it's love and we've just got to go through with it. There's no way out."

And now with this tragic suddenness the way out had come. I turned a little to look at Mary and she, feeling my eyes upon her, turned too. There was a smile on her lips.

"Why did you come here tonight? It must be awful for you."

She shrugged her shoulders.

"What could I do? I read the news in the evening paper while I was dressing. He'd asked me not to ring up the nursing home on account of his wife. It's death to me. Death. I had to come. We'd been engaged for a month. What excuse could I give Tom? I'm not supposed to have seen Gerrard for two years. Do you know that for twenty years we've written to one another every day?" Her lower lip trembled a little, but she bit it and for a moment her face was twisted to a strange grimace; then with a smile she pulled herself together. "He was everything I had in the world, but I couldn't let the party down, could I? He always said I had a social sense."

"Happily we shall break up early and you can go home."

"I don't want to go home. I don't want to be alone. I daren't cry because my eyes will get red and swollen, and we've got a lot of people lunching with us tomorrow. Will you come, by the way? I want an extra man. I must be in good form; Tom expects to get a commission for a portrait out of it."

"By George, you've got courage."

"D'you think so? I'm heartbroken, you know. I suppose that's what makes it easier for me. Gerrard would have liked me to put a good face on it. He would have appreciated the irony of the situation. It's the sort of thing he always thought the French novelists described so well."

# THE FOUR DUTCHMEN

THE Van Dorth Hotel at Singapore was far from grand. The bedrooms were dingy and the mosquito nets patched and darned; the bathhouses, all in a row and detached from the bedrooms, were dank and smelly. But it had character. The people who stayed there, masters of tramps whose round ended at Singapore, mining engineers out of a job and planters taking a holiday, to my mind bore a more romantic air than the smart folk, globe trotters, government officials and their wives, wealthy merchants, who gave luncheon parties at the Europe and played golf and danced and were fashionable. The Van Dorth had a billiard room, with a table with a threadbare cloth, where ships' engineers and clerks in insurance offices played snooker. The dining room was large and bare and silent. Dutch families on the way to Sumatra ate stolidly through their dinner without exchanging a word with one another, and single gentlemen on a business trip from Batavia devoured a copious meal while they intently read their paper. On two days a week there was rijs-tafel and then a few residents of Singapore who had a fancy for this dish came for tiffin. The Van Dorth

Hotel should have been a depressing place, but somehow it wasn't; its quaintness saved it. It had a faint aroma of something strange and half forgotten. There was a scrap of garden facing the street where you could sit in the shade of trees and drink cold beer. In that crowded and busy city, though motors whizzed past and rickshaws passed continuously, the coolies' feet pattering on the road and their bells ringing, it had the remote peacefulness of a corner of Holland. It was the third time I had stayed at the Van Dorth. I had been told about it first by the skipper of a Dutch tramp, the SS. Utrecht, on which I had travelled from Merauke in New Guinea to Macassar. The journey took the best part of a month, since the ship stopped at a number of islands in the Malay Archipelago, the Aru and the Kei Islands, Banda-Neira, Amboina and others of which I have even forgotten the names, sometimes for an hour or two, sometimes for a day, to take on or discharge cargo. It was a charming, monotonous and diverting trip. When we dropped anchor the agent came out in his launch, and generally the Dutch Resident, and we gathered on deck under the awning and the captain ordered beer. The news of the island was exchanged for the news of the world. We brought papers and mail. If we were staying long enough the Resident asked us to dinner and, leaving the ship in charge of the second officer, we all (the captain, the chief officer, the engineer, the supercargo and I) piled into the launch and went ashore. We spent a merry evening. These little islands, one so like another, allured my fancy just because I knew that I should never see them again. It made them strangely unreal, and as we sailed away and they vanished into the sea and sky it was only by an effort of the imagination that I could persuade myself that they did not with my last glimpse of them cease to exist.

But there was nothing illusive, mysterious or fantastic about the captain, the chief officer, the chief engineer and the supercargo. Their solidity was amazing. They were the four fattest men I ever saw. At first I had great difficulty in telling them apart, for though one, the supercargo, was dark and the others were fair, they looked astonishingly alike. They were all big, with large round bare red faces, with large fat arms and large fat legs and large fat bellies. When they went ashore they buttoned up their stengah-shifters and then their great double chins bulged over the collars and they looked as though they would choke. But generally they wore them unbuttoned. They sweated freely and wiped their shiny faces with bandanas and vigorously fanned themselves with palm-leaf fans.

It was a treat to see them at tiffin. Their appetites were enormous. They had rijs-tafel every day and each seemed to vie with the other how high he could pile his plate. They loved it hot and strong.

"In dis country you can't eat a ting onless it's tasty," said the skipper.

"De only way to keep yourself up in dis country is to eat hearty," said the chief.

They were the greatest friends, all four of them; they were like schoolboys together, playing absurd little pranks with one another. They knew each other's jokes by heart and no sooner did one of them start the familiar lines than he would splutter with laughter so violently, the heavy shaking laughter of the fat man, that he could not go on, and then the others began to laugh too. They rolled about in their chairs, and grew redder and redder, hotter and hotter, till the skipper shouted for beer, and each, gasping but happy, drank his bottle in one enchanted draught. They had been on this run together for five years and when a little time before the chief officer had been offered a ship of his own he refused it. He would not leave his companions. They had made up their minds that when the first of them retired they would all retire.

"All friends and a good ship. Good grub and good beer. Vot can a sensible man vant more?"

At first they were a little standoffish with me. Although the ship had accommodation for half a dozen passengers, they did not often get any, and never one whom they did not know. I was a stranger and a foreigner. They liked their bit of fun and did not want anyone to interfere with it. But they were all of them fond of bridge, and on occasion the chief and the engineer had duties that prevented one or the other from playing. They were willing to put up with me when they discovered that I was ready to make a fourth whenever I was wanted. Their bridge was as incredibly fantastic as they were. They played for infinitesimal stakes, five cents a hundred: they did not want to win one another's money, they said, it was the game they liked. But what a game! Each was wildly determined to play the hand and hardly one was dealt without at least a small slam being declared. The rule was that if you could get a peep at somebody else's cards you did and if you could get away with a revoke you told your partner when there was no danger it could be claimed and you both roared with laughter till the tears rolled down your fat cheeks. But if your partner had insisted on taking the bid away from you and had called a grand slam on five spades to the queen, whereas you were positive that on your seven little diamonds you could have made it easily, you could always score him off by redoubling without a trick in your hand. He went down two or three thousand and the glasses on the table danced with the laughter that shook your opponents.

I could never remember their difficult Dutch names, but knowing them anonymously as it were, only by the duties they performed, as one knows the characters, Pantaloon, Harlequin and Punchinello, of the old Italian comedy, added grotesquely to their drollery. The mere sight of them, all four together, set you laughing, and I think they got a good deal of amusement from the astonishment they caused in strangers. They boasted that they were the four most famous Dutchmen in the East Indies. To me not the least comic part of them was their serious side. Sometimes late at night, when they had given up all pretence of still wearing their uniforms, and one or the other of them lay by my side on a long chair in a pyjama jacket and a sarong, he would grow sentimental. The chief engineer, due to retire soon, was meditating marriage with a widow whom he had met when last he was home and spending the rest of his life in a little town with old red brick houses on the shores of the Zuyder Zee. But the captain was very susceptible to the charms of the native girls and his thick English became almost unintelligible from emotion when he described to me the effect they had on him. One of these days he would buy himself a house on the hills in Java and marry a pretty little Javanese. They were so small and so gentle and they made no noise, and he would dress her in silk sarongs and give her gold chains to wear round her neck and gold bangles to put on her arms. But the chief mocked him.

"Silly all dat is. Silly. She goes mit all your friends and de houseboys and everybody. By de time you retire, my dear, vot you'll vant vill be a nurse, not a vife."

"Me?" cried the skipper. "I shall vant a vife ven I'm eighty!"

He had picked up a little thing last time the ship was at Macassar and as we approached that port he began to be all of a flutter. The chief officer shrugged fat and indulgent shoulders. The captain was always losing his head over one brazen hussy after another, but his passion never survived the interval between one stop at a port and the next, and then the chief was called in to smooth out the difficulties that ensued. And so it would be this time.

"De old man suffers from fatty degeneration of de heart. But so long as I'm dere to look after him not much harm comes of it. He vastes his money and dat's a pity, but as long as he's got it to vaste, vhy shouldn't he?"

The chief officer had a philosophic soul.

At Macassar then I disembarked and bade farewell to my four fat friends.

"Make another journey with us," they said. "Come back next year or the year after. You'll find us all here just the same as ever."

A good many months had passed since then and I had wandered through more than one strange land. I had been to Bali and Java and Sumatra; I had been to Cambodia and Annam; and now, feeling as though I were home again, I sat in the garden of the Van Dorth Hotel. It was cool in the very early morning and having had breakfast I was looking at back numbers of the Straits Times to find out what had been happening in the world since last I had been within reach of papers. Nothing very much. Suddenly my eyes caught a headline: The Utrecht Tragedy. Supercargo and Chief Engineer. Not Guilty. I read the paragraph carelessly and then I sat up. The Utrecht was the ship of my four fat Dutchmen and apparently the supercargo and the chief engineer had been on trial for murder. It couldn't be my two fat friends. The names were given, but the names meant nothing to me. The trial had taken place in Batavia. No details were given in this paragraph; it was only a brief announcement that after the judges had considered the speeches of the prosecution and of the defence their verdict was as stated. I was astounded. It was incredible that the men I knew could have committed a murder. I could not find out who had been murdered. I looked through back numbers of the paper. Nothing.

I got up and went to the manager of the hotel, a genial Dutchman, who spoke admirable English, and showed him the paragraph.

"That's the ship I sailed on. I was in her for nearly a month. Surely these fellows aren't the men I knew. The men I knew were enormously fat."

"Yes, that's right," he answered. "They were celebrated all through the Dutch East Indies, the four fattest men in the service. It's been a terrible thing. It made a great sensation. And they were friends. I knew them all. The best fellows in the world."

"But what happened?"

He told me the story and answered my horrified questions. But there were things I wanted to know that he couldn't tell me. It was all confused. It was unbelievable. What actually had happened was only conjecture. Then someone claimed the manager's attention and I went back to the garden. It was getting hot now and I went up to my room. I was strangely shattered.

It appeared that on one of the trips the captain

took with him a Malay girl that he had been carrying on with and I wondered if it was the one he had been so eager to see when I was on board. The other three had been against her coming—what did they want with a woman in the ship? it would spoil everything—but the captain insisted and she came. I think they were all jealous of her. On that journey they didn't have the fun they generally had. When they wanted to play bridge the skipper was dallying with the girl in his cabin; when they touched at a port and went ashore the time seemed long to him till he could get back to her. He was crazy about her. It was the end of all their larks. The chief officer was more bitter against her than anybody: he was the captain's particular chum, they had been shipmates ever since they first came out from Holland; more than once high words passed between them on the subject of the captain's infatuation. Presently those old friends spoke to one another only when their duties demanded it. It was the end of the good fellowship that had so long obtained between the four fat men. Things went from bad to worse. There was a feeling among the junior officers that something untoward was pending. Uneasiness. Tension. Then one night the ship was aroused by the sound of a shot and the screams of the Malay girl. The supercargo and the chief engineer tumbled out of their bunks and they found the captain, a revolver in his hand, at the door of the chief officer's cabin. He pushed past them and went on deck. They entered and found the chief officer dead and the girl cowering behind the door. The captain had found them in bed together and had killed the chief. How he had discovered what was going on didn't seem to be known, nor what was the meaning of the intrigue. Had the chief induced the girl to come to his cabin in order to get back on the captain, or had she, knowing his ill will and anxious to placate him, lured him to become her lover? It was a mystery that would never be solved. A dozen possible explanations flashed across my mind. While the engineer and the supercargo were in the cabin, horror-struck at the sight before them, another shot was heard. They knew at once what had happened. They rushed up the companion. The captain had gone to his cabin and blown his brains out. Then the story grew dark and enigmatic. Next morning the Malay girl was nowhere to be found and when the second officer who had taken command of the ship reported this to the supercargo, the supercargo said: "She's probably jumped overboard. It's the best thing she could have done. Good riddance to bad rubbish." But one of the sailors on the watch, just before dawn, had seen the supercargo and the chief engineer carry something up on deck, a bulky package, about the size of a native woman, look about them to see that they were unobserved, and drop it overboard; and it was said all over the ship that these two to avenge their friends had sought the girl out in her cabin and strangled her and flung her body into the sea. When the ship arrived at Macassar they were arrested and taken to Batavia to be tried for murder. The evidence was flimsy and they were acquitted. But all through the East Indies they knew that the supercargo and the chief engineer had executed justice on the trollop who had caused the death of the two men they loved.

And thus ended the comic and celebrated friendship of the four fat Dutchmen.